THE TURKISH ORDER

KEITH D. KIZZIE

MMXVIII

DORRANCE
PUBLISHING CO
EST. 1920
PITTSBURGH, PENNSYLVANIA 15238

Dorrance Publishing Co
585 Alpha Drive
Pittsburgh, PA 15238
Visit our website at www.dorrancebookstore.com

ISBN: 978-1-4809-4961-4
eISBN: 978-1-4809-4938-6

Dedicated to the tears

—Mast Women—

Forest, Part I

Stroll trail, holding hands break, smiles, teeth, running glee, an approving glance, chance. The toddler opens his gate, the smell, the wild, the free.

Curves of leaves, breeze weaves, flicker, atop ashone, beneath ashade, the prickly points, air blanket cascades gently down, unfolds and lays.

Falling with slow drift, first touches mist, kneads in the air, kiss, binding trees' shoulders, arms and fists.

Mist, covered and stirring, the pulsing lush, trust, thick, flowing pass the height of man. Limbs engulfed, surface must, Earth skin touch.

Down so slowly, an ancient army march. The mix, an endless parade processions, hill after hill, paths, twix, twist, twigs, flows lust.

Rubs, knots, crevice, bark? Brown surrounds trunks, the living shrubs, onto the deck. In and around swirls homeless willed, inhaled, pushed into and onto new worlds or of the billions scream killed.

"I don't believe you. How do you know? You said the room was dark…you always exaggerate and you might be lying now. Did you taste it? Did you smell it? Was it really different?"

"No, PNi, this was it."

PNi turns her eyes down and back to the door.

"Anything, but eye contact now," she thinks.

PNi will not show MKi what MKi so doubts. This feeling of commitment and devotion will be said, but not with the eyes.

"I will always be a part of you just like you are of me."

MKi, a second ago, could control her breathing, chest heaving and pressure behind her lobes. No more, the weeping adrenaline rushes out from deep within her. MKi's neck relaxes, she lowers her head; her skin feels new, and she cannot resist any longer the spirit to gape her mouth and to make sounds of sorrow, joy and fear at the same time. MKi's words are loud, but not audible thru the teary sobs, sweaty face and mucus taste. Before she can be heard, PNi approaches her in a hurry, touching her with hands, first on both shoulders. She pulls-in and leans until their thighs and breasts press.

"Mki still does not know."

"So long since we have been close."

PNi's body is so comforting, but tense. Tense and ripe for what she is expecting to come next. PNi breaths along the neck, up the back of the ear, gently passes her hand over MKi's forehead, controlling her matted hair, out of her eyes and behind her ears. The first kiss entered slowly, MKi's and PNi's eyes open. MKi, full of doubt, looking to see if she will be alone. PNi withholding wondering if she should doubt also.

The second kiss pressed hard together.

"Was this goodbye?"

The thought scores deeper, and the once racing heart seeks more of a normal rhythm as MKi satisfies herself in knowing that this time will be forever.

PNi knows that MKi, so feeling and expressive, does not know, even after much confession, that she, PNi, whose heart may not be as big, loves more. PNi will not delay any longer for fear that MKi will believe that it is over. Once that feeling is accepted, it's much easier to get there again, and she will not risk losing Mki.

"His blood is real, MKi and he doesn't get me without you."

❧

Out of control, the mind protects, neglects, heart, sweats, gets, gets, gets, ah…

❧

Can it, would it, will it, the doubt sprints, rent?
    She, be, tee, key, see my insides, dance, glow, glee.
    Next, plex, let, let, let… a mess.
    Undeterred, first, skirt, dirt, flirt, flirt, flirt.
    Surely, purely, curly, mesh, text, not sex.
    Need, need, need, bleed.

❧

"Don' t tell me that the recital is pointless," Zyi aims after completing the recital.

"It is," replied Cmi. "The manual screwdriver will, in the not so far off, be an obsolete mystery."

"What does that prove?"

Cmi, without thinking countered, just to counter, forcing Zyi, if Zyi wished, to make the point without really offering a defense.

"It proves that what appears to be mundane, slight, routine and or insignificant, yet full of utility in the present, stands a good chance of being shortcut, programmed, automized or replaced by another tool or process, in this case, leaving the screwdriver obsolete. Once obsolete and as time goes by, fewer and fewer know or remember the screwdriver, hence the mystery."

Resignation dulled over Cmi's countenance like a long, thick grey cloud passing over the clear part of the sky and the sunny day's sun.

"Hence...," Cmi thought and started to chime in with sarcasm, but Zyi matched Cmi's voice while turning to make passing eye contact in unison with Cmi.

"...the mystery," finishing Cmi's reply that was nothing but that.

"A reply, all the same and with a certain cadence," Zyi thought.

"Cmi has some fight," a noted thought as Zyi went back to the task at hand.

"Okay, but it seems so..." Cmi couldn't find the words, especially after yielding the first spar to Zyi.

"Don't worry about it, Cmi," Zyi interjected. "These are my expressions, my thoughts, my rhythm now and right here, Cmi'," Zyi, almost asking, conveyed to Cmi.

"Your..." Cmi started again and was again met by Zyi.

"...expressions," guessing which of the descriptors that Cmi would use first; Zyi masked Cmi's voice and finished the thought.

"...my thoughts, rhythm, and now and right here."

Zyi left it for Cmi to express understanding, inquire further or further resign in an empty challenge or by changing the subject, the later impossible.

"A little understanding, my dear friend..."

Zyi knew and thought, "...just a little, Cmi. Give it a chance." Zyi dropped, again, not so much asking. "It may appear to be but a screwdriver, a dagger you would not forget."

"It's not a notched dagger," Zyi offered to further the point.

Cmi, having been bested twice, looked to think about how to get Zyi to make the point, but to do it in such a way as to not make it seem so one side dominated. "What is it then?" Cmi thought with true curiosity, but with venom of resent of being defeated and almost forced to have Zyi, now, dictate.

"It's a meditation."

"How do I communicate this to Cmi?" Zyi's mental consciousness asked. "I don't want to alienate Cmi."

When two of nearly balanced standing have to communicate, the how is not the problem. Then again, the true grandmasters always seemed to have a little extra, not just the message, to offer. This occurs especially when the message can be around a tense issue.

"Please? You and your family and faithful friends, and loyals of business, etc. say, 'I am going to kill you,'...nothing of this sort or directness does nothing but play the evil version of God," Zyi's thoughts continued. "Not even God would be so callous in condemning the inequity."

Zyi began with a little risk, "I say this without injury, insult or intent to degrade or disrespect."

"I'm sorry," thought Zyi. "I am so sorry, and yes, Cmi, it is a meditation," Zyi passed the thought sounding as if the thought cured for over a thousand years.

"Yes," Zyi re-confirmed.

Turning the head, Cmi tried to make direct and full pleading eye contact, glanced up and down Zyi taking a measure just to be sure. Like in most glances, the measure was already concluded in Cmi's mind.

Zyi was pretty sure, and there was no indication of doubt in the demeanor, movements, stances or gestures.

"Does there need to be something else said about it?" Zyi responded. Cmi, in the recently familiar confounded state, did not think about how to respond now thinking that Zyi would out-respond and steal the momentum again.

"Well," thought Cmi, "bring it home, after all that we have been through, told, taught and trained."

"You have to have questions like I do Zyi?" Cmi's voice trailing with the balance of frustration and taunting. "What about that time when it was just the two of us in that so-called training event? After all the fasting, traveling, dealing with every extreme weather conditions from the tropics to the Arctic. What about the..." Cmi looked for the words, the mouth moving, but not stuttering... "What about the, what they called the Keepers and the one we came across half way through those savannah lands? Let's review what happened, Zyi," Cmi, not in full confrontation mode, but wanted to make a point.

"Yeah, let's review," Cmi responded and continued. "We were barely into the trek, and you were showing signs of cracking. I am proud you made it, and I was glad that you made it with me to see the Keepers."

⟨※⟩

Approaching the Keeper, Zyi and Cmi, had been on their own, except for the intermittent encounters with the other Keepers and trial events along the way. They knew they were close, but had no apparent signs of the proper location. Knowing and finding locations was one of the essential aspects of the treks and their training. They keep moving, instinctively, becoming more cautious; a sign that their skills of location were improving. Cmi reached back outstretching the left arm, below the waist, palm outward and fingers fully extended downward signaling Zyi not to stop, but to move to the hand and no further. When they were together, the Keeper did not riddle or waste energy or time.

"You know why we are here," the Keeper said with impending and began. "They came to the place where the carnal energies flowed." The Keeper getting their attention. "The Ns knew nothing about the spots. Some of the spots were surface spots, some were sub-surface in or beneath the ponds, lakes, streams, rivers or oceans. Some of the hills, cliffs, caves or peaks, and some were aerials. How to find them?" the Keeper threw in just to continue for emphasis.

Zyi joked in eye contact with Cmi, but without words, "How did we find you?"

Cmi looked disapprovingly and then turned back to the Keeper who continued with an indifference that did not say indifference.

"In the past, explorers at first considered a cult, a silly one at that, began to seek the spots through wandering and reporting. The Wanders or Wanderers or Ones as they came to be called used techniques, maps and journals that were so crude. They wanted to have recorded proof of the spots and wanted everyone to be able to interpret the maps and benefit from the spots' various energy forms. This planet is a sphere, and what do we know about spheres? What is it the architects and physicists seem so pre-occupied with: the axis or axes?"

The Keeper continued not entertaining and not fully reciting, "This sphere has major and minor axes that we generally use, but in fact, how many axes are there? If anyone were to create something special, something enduring, something because of its power, was for the few trusted, prepared and able to manage the power and to use the power in the proper cause, yes, maps are useful, but maps predicated on emphasizing certain parts of the sphere obviously and by definition de-emphasize other parts of the same sphere. And if that same someone was to conceal certain really dominant axis or points along this axis or axes, the infinity of the axes prevails."

Fast after the Keeper's last statement and without conscious thought, Zyi stirred, breaking the grip of the situation on the three of them. Cmi stayed focused on the Keeper, but acknowledged Zyi stirring that was not intended to interlope in or on the Keeper's words.

Zyi reflected, "Before the flood, before the bend and break, take, take, take, the illusion of falsehood lies and fakes, interjects with ruckus, faints, distractions and decoys in useless attempt to bury the truth."

The Keeper continued, not allowing the truth to be buried, pushed through, on auto-pilot and having seen this before, showing Zyi that that stir was ineffectual as others will be as well.

"Think of every location held in esteem, and think of the axes on the sphere. Is there a relationship on the surface or parts of the surfaces on where the axes appear to break through the surfaces, or are there patterns of the intersections of the axes?"

Cmi reached over as Zyi sat near and steadied Zyi again with the left hand knowing that Cmi was trying to reject the Keeper's words, but could not reject the impossible math of the axes and the sphere.

"Keeper," Cmi snuck in knowing that it was not time to talk, but felt it necessary to ask. Ask to further understand, but to also ask to help Zyi to get back too.

"The places of esteem…," stating and questioning.

"I know what you are saying," Zyi closer to confirming, "the seats of power, the magnificent cathedrals, the capitals, universities, the natural wonders, and the economic centers are the places of esteem?"

"What do you think, what do you know, and what do you believe? The "so-called" natural catastrophes were indeed co-dependent and directly related to the spots," the Keeper concluded.

"I think…," Cmi started.

"I may see you on your return," the Keeper cut in.

Cmi cut in also in thought, but knew not to dare in word. "On your return?" Cmi immediately felt the imbalance and discomfort of the thought of having to complete the trek and then return to this particular Keeper.

"From the tropic to the Arctic, my ass. I will be damned," Cmi almost vocalized.

"You know he is talking philosophy. Philosophy is not important until you have children…"

"I don't have children," Cmi squeezed in.

"Shut up trout," Zyi shot back while staying with the Keeper…

"…after that, philosophy is…"

The eye contact was a mix of, "okay, the humor of deep friends, but also I am going to get you for that."

"…everything."

"Give me what you got because I don't know when or if we will pass this way again. There are unknowns out there, Keeper," Cmi finally let out.

"I like you, Cmi," the Keeper offered as a consolation, turning to take measure of Zyi's response to the acknowledgement, knowing that Zyi was understanding that Cmi did not.

"No need to continue here. I have to prepare for the next ones," the Keeper closed the door on Cmi's rebellious soft push back.

Zyi, without taking eyes off the Keeper, disappearing much like the appearance, reached with the right hand. As Zyi's hand moved toward Cmi, Zyi, without thinking about it, sensually exploded, detecting the exact exacts of the body that was about to be touched. Zyi met Cmi's abdomen's side, right outside of the frontal belly and belly button and above the hip. The touch, rode up Cmi's side into the curve of Cmi's body, calming them both. The absence of wind, maybe not the turn of the world's simple touch, reduced Cmi to the finality of the situation.

PNi starts on her own to prepare as she knows that she will have to make the case for MKi.

"Oh, yeah, that saying about the hardest part of a 1,000 miles journey is the first step. Those that say that know nothing to very little about the last step," PNi recited to herself in brief reflection.

It wasn't the task at hand, but more concern if the task at hand once completed would yield what was needed.

"We are inseparable and should be understood to be so in his eyes," MKi planned.

"It is not that we are inseparable. Inseparable, but together we offer so much more to the purpose and progress of The Order. The Turkish Order." Almost in questioning thought, MKi wondered about her place and her place with PNi. In existence and history, allowing a brief moment of freedom from what she had been taught, trained and confirmed to believe that once committed and trained, her purpose was clear, and her existence would be dedicated to the reasons for necessity of and furthering of The Order and The Order's reason and many reasons for doing what it does.

"He is so damn perfect," MKi challenged to herself. "I hate perfection. Do I hate perfection? Where do these guys come from?" MKi rhetorically asked aloud, stops her rambling thoughts for a long moment while she moves across the semi-improved encampment's foot-worn paths. With no visual focus and still moving, the questions continue. "Are they serious? Are the stories and the secrets true?" Mki regained focus and bought back in.

"Well, we are inseparable and if he doesn't know it by now, he soon will."

—Classical Heart—

"Welcome to my heart…Welcome to my wants and needs…Wel…
come to my hopes and fears…And of you…so many dreams"

The cadence of the melody was energy for RNi.

"It seems to fit," the thought was natural and it was accepted to her
without pause. RNi ran on. She knew this was it, literally the run of
her life. "Welcome to my wants….," RNi's arms swung, without
thought, without hesitation, without need of command or response to
command. Her legs thinking to carry the day in this endeavor moved
with intuition, searching her mind for what is to come next. RNi inhaled, shortly filling her ready lungs with oxygen and vaporous material, digested for her purpose and reflected.

"The legs are not yours," she recalled, her Teacher only saying it
once and then only under the most felt duress.

Now, RNi knew the Teacher from before, her way in doing and
showing and not saying, but short of a legectomy, there was just no
other way to communicate to the learner that the "Legs are not yours."

RNi moved on, almost gliding along the path and course for the
Proven. It was a run and not a race because the nature of the finish was

more like a run than a race with a finish line where contestants finish 1st, 2nd and 3rd and so on.

"In my world," the Teacher explained "if your legs come to fail you, like the trust of a long friend, you may as well cut them off and live a docile life."

"Her world" in another half-a-step, and RNi thought, "Now it was her world," and she knew her legs were not hers.

She knew that she would have to separate herself from at first the whisper, the whispers of the legs. The whispers of foreboding of what was to come if RNi persisted on doing what it is that she was doing in the Proven. The whispers did not mind, respect, or compliment in any way the cadence RNi was enjoying. It was still there, like a stroking of the mane, invigorating, reassuring and sedating-the melody, the cadence.

"Welcome to My Heart…"

Her mind relaxed again in the rhythm of her stride and turned down the whispers as it would the later voices of the legs, the shouts and the screams. RNi knew the legs but also knew that they would scream like strangers, alone and in the grasp of danger before the Proven was done.

"The legs are not yours," RNi now knew, even if spoken only once to the group of preparers at that time, was the essence of the lessons for the Proven and the essential part of her mental and physical ability and preparation for the Proven. Knowing was different; RNi reflected back to her days of training. It was pre-ordained that only a small number of the ones preparing for the Proven would detect the seriousness and finality of the Teacher's words.

The Teacher's delivery left no immediate clues to the importance or gravity of the phrase. As the Teacher gathered the preparers, she spoke just long enough for those whose interest and minds tended to wane, to let their minds dial the teacher out and to review other things.

The Teacher's words at first were very encouraging to Wbyny, one of the favored preparers for the Proven. Wbyny listened as the Teacher, who seemed to be looking downward in thought as well as in direction, her gaze moved just past the knees of the group of preparers as she spoke seeming to be kind of casual with her address to the group.

Wbyny, instead of continuing to listen, thought in slow motion. The slow motion pleased her because it allowed her to remain disengaged from what the Teacher was saying.

Wbyny thought, "I will ask her more about that later."

The Teacher continued to move by turning to the other side of the group and said, "The Proven is purposeful and purifying…"

"Blah, blah, blah," Wbyny said under her breath so slightly that she was sure that no one could have understood what she was saying even if the audible change was noticed. "The Proven is telling…," RNi could spell the words backwards and sideways in both directions in her mind as the Teacher spoke and before the Teacher finished a sentence. Even though RNi was utterly exhausted, she fixed herself to the Teacher, familiar with the Teacher's forward-like lean and downward roaming gaze as she spoke.

"The Proven is purifying," Wbyny heard the Teacher say but the sounds were in the back of her ear and mind. The Teacher continued to speak but raised her eyes and head without attempting to synchronize her next words with the indistinguishable vocal murmurs coming from the direction of Wbyny.

Somehow, it was in that second, the Teacher's words, "The legs are not yours" were passed right out to the preparers.

There was a noticeable up-tick in the volume of the Teacher's voice since her voice was moving directly at the ear and eye level of the group of the preparers. The Teacher took quick inventory as she continued to speak about the ties between the Proven and their social organizations. RNi's eyes motionless in their sockets at that brief second, except for a slight downward, response to the constant heaving of her upper body as she breathed deeply in exhaustion. The Teacher was speaking. She raised her head and continued to roam through the group with her vision.

RNi exhaled, recalibrated her gaze to meet the Teacher's eyes. The Teacher's inventory counted RNi as attentive, and the Teacher's voice and face glided away from Rni's immediate line of sight.

RNi remained, having to just tune-into the words a little more as the Teacher revealed her face and eyes to the rest of the group on her left as RNi and the others, on the Teacher's right, could now see the Teacher's upper profile. RNi continued to reflect on her days of training. As the Teacher turned, the Teacher said, "The legs are not yours, yet we have come on our legs to this place and time."

RNi took note of her ear and the taunt skin of her neck, skin stretched over the slender muscular part of the Teacher's vessel. RNi heard, "Social beings, places and organizations move toward a wholesome collective identity."

The Teacher continued to speak as she began to slowly swing back her gaze to the part of the group on her right. As she came to the point in the group where she knew RNi was standing and breathing, the Teacher did not focus. The Teacher caught the blurred stare of RNi and glided pass her.

"RNi has the courage," she thought behind her words as she took inventory of Wbyny.

Wbyny was looking at the Teacher's face and eyes and scratching along the skin on her triceps with her opposite hand. Wbyny seemed to be looking through the Teacher's eyes, and to some point beyond where the Teacher was standing. The Teacher, after moving her line of vision just enough pass Wbyny, not to arouse Wbyny or give her any indication of what the Teacher was thinking, the Teacher slowly started to lower her gaze back to the area around the preparers' legs.

"Wbyny is full of talent, she was perfect, but that was then, now," the Teacher thought. "That maggot may not last."

The Teacher thought quickly about the size of this group of preparers. "This group was about the normal size of the other groups of preparers."

"The size of the social organizations is always relative…," she continued to lecture the preparers.

Wbyny may as well have just walked away from the group because her attention and real focus was on recovering from her exhaustion, getting the sweat and dirt and grit removed from her bodily crevices and off her skin and out of her hair and from underneath her nails.

Another pass around their legs, the Teacher's inventory was complete. RNi allowed the statement to be heard in the frontal part of her head; it didn't seem to come in through the ears.

"That was it," she knew it intuitively as the words slowly, one by one with deliberation, entered her head, spread across and into her tissue and soaked-in and gathered again with force and intensity as their meaning exploded into her being as the words themselves disappeared with the blast. Their remnants plastered inside of RNi.

"One of the parts of the many parts of the foundations of the organization is the ability to nourish itself," the Teacher said.

"Lha, OTi and RNi are ready," she thought. "The inventory was complete."

RNi recalled how she thought about it as the Teacher, without any inflection, hesitation or any other indication, continued to talk as if she did not just release the special words. RNi later was informed thru the selection process that that was when the Teacher acknowledged RNi as one of the preparers that would go on and possibly make it into the Proven.

"There is only one way to be Proven: you push yourself into an outer body-like existence and when you reach that state, you remain there. This way you not only lose your legs, you lose everything. Your body is no longer yours, but together you move through the time and space almost without effort until you become Proven."

∽

The patterned and solid color garbs cling and sing in the head force wind as the tribe's women full-round about to birth the ones that may one day be Proven. History's memories flowed through the thoughts of RNi's mother as she conjured the images of the countless times that expectant mothers set out to bring their small ones into existence with the rhythm of the run, the cadence of the songs, the sun, rain and wind-rumbled hum of bare feet striding upon earth, snow, rock, sand, grass or ocean salted shore.

RNi's mother, in the splendor of the memories of the practice, blinked and slowed the flow of the images in her thoughts to preserve the feeling and to fully harness the power of the recollection.

Sometimes in small groups, sometimes in large groups, sometimes the expectant ones set out alone, especially in the final days of expectancy, to be sure that the little ones felt and experienced and were born into it. For some incalculable reason, RNi's mother recalled a modest group, trailing with good pace and traditional head dress, complementing the colors and patterns of their vibrant body wraps, shoals, long skirts and pigmented lips. They moved as the head wind pressed the garments against their full bellies, legs, some knees, nipples and breast.

"Welcome to my dreams"

The rhythm of the song stayed in her head as she pushed farther along the course. There was meaning in the song. There was power in its cadence, and the power was becoming hers. Now RNi paused in her thinking of the Proven. "Dreams?" she asked herself as the cadence continued in the back of her thoughts. She felt her body move into what was like another level of performance. It felt reassuring in that she did not feel fatigue, but invigoration. RNi's feet felt light and springy. Her legs were whispering, but as she moved up the long incline, the legs responded with the adequate push to allow her to pulse up the incline with only still a whisper from the legs to slow down. Her skin felt the air as it passed over her exposed limbs, frontal abdomen, back and neck. The air was cooling and refreshing. The air pulled her hair back in a short train cooling her head with a tingly sensation. RNi's lungs were in tune with the song she breathed in harmony with the song.

"Welcome," was pronounced in song, carrying the "W" sound with the inhalation, and the sound of the word "come" with the exhalation. She knew that she could recall the words of the song and slow them down or speed them up whenever she felt that she needed, but the version of the song that she recalled had its own rhythm.

"Why was this the rhythm for her to have recalled?" RNi thought. After all, she only overheard it being sung once by her lover.

RNi recalled that time with her lover as she glided along the course not passing and not being passed. She was alone.

Her lover moved out of their long held embrace and prepared for the coming events. RNi relaxed, pleased about her relationship with her lover. She reflected on how her lover responded to her inner being without even knowing it. As RNi held that thought of amusement, the words of the song began to become detectable to her consciousness. Now she realized that the lover had been singing the song for a little while, so she tuned into the words, the tone and the cadence. The lover, without any ratification of RNi's presence, continued to move about quietly filling the spaces with the words:

"Welcome to my heart, welcome to my dreams…"

She did not know it, but the words had never been rehearsed, sung or spoken. Her lover in the midst of preparing for the coming events, still a little warmed from the embrace of RNi, let the words pick themselves and their timing:

"Welcome to my hopes and fears…"

RNi did not shy away in her thoughts. Her lover was sharing, again, so she relaxed her body, turned to watch and catch glimpses of her lover as the lover got ready to leave. RNi heard the words, felt their meaning, knew their place and importance in the life of her lover and was gently overcome. RNi knew that her lover would not return to her embrace this minute, this hour nor in this day, nor would she see her lover's face until they met again later that day or on another day. Her lover crossed her field of sight once more, and then the volume of the song started to fade as the lover moved away from her and toward the outside.

❧

The crackle of the separating pebbles under the weight of another participant's strides, rushed into her consciousness.

"Someone was near me," the thought passed in and out of RNi, registering affirmation that the competition was unfolding as she thought that it would.

She opened her vision, no longer short and narrow in reflection, but wide and long as she continued through the desert part of the Proven. Not too far in front of her, RNi saw the moving mass of one of the other participants. Exactly 18 hours later, as the sun began to be a source of heat and not a morning jewel, RNi passed the participant.

"Would she see her again?" RNi thought.

Not only did she wonder if the other participant would catch her in the competition, but would she ever see her again in life. RNi knew only one of those conclusions could be true. The Proven was only finished by one.

"What training had this competitor undergone, and why was my training seeming superior at this point?" RNi took account of the passing.

The training for the Proven was developed through research, trial and error of the ages with the Order for ones who have reached a point of being able to be Proven. The early civilizations needed to be able to run. Run fast when needed and to run long was quickly realized as a means of survival. Beastly prey had to be run down in all the various environmental settings around the sphere. Beings could not overpower the beasts, so they had to outlast them. After scaring or wounding the beasts, the beings chased the beasts until the beasts were exhausted. Beings were recognized for what seemed to be an innate ability for some to run better than others. The best runners were held in esteem and given privilege in the being groups.

When beings began the violent era, the ability to run was again obviously beneficial. The leaders learned the benefits of having good runners to out maneuver and to strike against their opponents. When larger groups came to gather for conflicts, the ability to send messengers on foot was critical in combat. Groups began to look to the innate runners as a separate sect of beings. The runners were important, but it was not so easily learned or accepted by everyone. RNi recalled the teachers' many lectures on the history of the Proven and how it made a difference. RNi recalled the story of Vgi.

⟋⟍

Vgi, stunned, stared back at her father, wondering, "Was he afraid for his own life and the lives of the rest of the family, or did he believe that she deserved to be killed by those that presumed her guilt?"

Prior to the family arriving at this state of destitution through her many feats of endurance and participation to sustain and protect the organization, Vgi was previously richly admired by the others in the community. It was widely known that she was a treasured and valuable member of the society. Her running prowess came to the fore at an early time in her life. Vgi was not an innate runner, but at the early age of five, the others ran and watched astonished as she outlasted a mid-sized young beast that was minimally wounded and sprinting off for safety.

During the chase, the young beast did not hesitate when faced with a broad, briskly moving river. The beast bound over the remainder of the land and plunged into the straits determined to escape the hunting party. Vgi could not swim yet, and everyone knew it, but did not hesitate in her approach to the river as well. The more experienced hunters quickly converged on Vgi, pulled her as she was fully submerged, yet still hurriedly moving forward. They got her out of the shallow depths and assisted her with haste to the other side. Vgi never lost focus of the beast, the river water blurring her tracking vision as the beast instinctively twisted and thrust its body out and away from the hunters. The waters sprayed, sprinkled and ran back to the river as the beast hurried away in muddy pulls of desperate survival. The hands that held her across the straits now started to open and release Vgi. The last hand flicked open hesitantly. Hesitantly to allow the girl the opportunity to demonstrate the ability to reach and to take a prominent place in the society. A place that no one in the long and wide lines of her family had achieved before. The last hands to release her belonged to her father. His face, unnoticeable to anyone who did not know him well, showed a slight welt in realizing the doubt, but his eyes held hope and resolve in knowing that it was now out of his hands. Vgi was released to seize this opportunity or to face failure and the code of dispensation of hunter runner failures. The others trailed in observation and duty. They would by code carry out whatever the conclusion required. With extreme focus on the fleeing young beast, Vgi was free and clear to either run the beast down or to fail.

Much time passed and much land was crossed. Many bodies of water were also crossed as Vgi learned to cross water bodies at the second river. At the second river, Vgi, while gaining on the beast, plunged-in. She reflected to how the others had pulled her through the first river, how it felt while submerged and the relief she felt in learning that she could not breathe for a time and still live. She understood water propulsion now and quickly gained on the beast in the many straits and bodies to follow, tuning and perfecting her technique with each encounter.

She thought, "This is fun and easy. Why couldn't Father swim more than he did?"

She, in all innocence, drew from the energy inherent in each of her accomplishments in the chase. When she crested a long rocky incline, noticing the blood seeping through the breaks in skin on her feet, something inside her took resource from that and the rest of her fed off of it. When Vgi now seemingly alone and away from the rest of the group, as they trailed at the proper distance, moved across the barren sandscape, her feet hardened and swelled, closing up the wounds and stopping the bleeding. She pushed on. As her trail of blood decreased, she found more and more of the blood of the wounded young beast. She gained on it. Her young limbs moved together while her gaze bore ahead to the withering prey. Instinctively, the young beast would not face the hunters. If the beast had, it could have easily turned on VGi and destroyed her. Instead, the young beast ran and ran. It ran through the morning turning away from, but keeping its right profile on the sun. It ran through the afternoon, evenings and night adjusting its course as it recalled its way back home. The small reflection of the sun, moon or stars in the dark eyes of the young beast as it attempted to push away from Vgi. Hearing the hurried and seemingly energy-filled pace of the one pursuing, the beast gathered itself once more and burst into stretch to escape. Later in life, Vgi did not recall this part of the chase as it was retold by the others, but she crossed the vastest, flattest open space in the land. At full speed, she and the beast were no longer in the context of the hunt, but in the context of overcoming the other.

The unbearable weight of the great trotting Phant at first touched, then landed, and without being noticed by the Phant, pushed down onto the outer shell of the nested eggs of the lesser animal. The lesser animal having laid the eggs there for safe keeping; the eggs, the ones never to be tested in life, to achieve, survive or to fail, never to know more than what the shell knew of the living realm. The Phant heavily galloped as best he could along the trail Vgi made as her streak across, over and through the land and forest did not go unnoticed or unfelt. The creatures of the land, water and tree took notice of her majestic pursuit. Some of the creatures received her energy and purpose. It rippled through them instantly, jolting them into response. They wanted to be with her in this undertaking. They wanted to be her in this undertaking. Some of the creatures just stood and watched Vgi move farther and farther away until she was completely out of sight. Other creatures walked in her wake while others chose to gallop, each using differing amounts of effort, strides and steps to keep the pace with Vgi.

FLG, one of the larger creatures, said to TLG, one of the other creatures, "I can't stop."

It was an admittance of its desire to stay with Vgi at all cost, and it seemed an admittance that communicated a sense of doom-fearing, great harm or sense of loss if the creature failed to stay with Vgi. The statement was not received or heard by TLG. TLG was too intent on remaining with Vgi. TLG felt the same way, but despite the presence of the abundant energy that spurned TLG to move and pursue Vgi, TLG's strides weakened. She redirected some of her concentration that was all previously reserved for focusing on Vgi to compensate for the waning in her legs. She felt a renewed surge and freshness. She felt at peace as the distance between her and the next group of creatures as well as the distance between her and Vgi increased. Her vision started to fade with a shading blur igniting and covering her eyes. The cover became darker and denser as it rolled from her outer eye, inward. Though her eyes remained fully open and she ran across the land, her vision was completely lost. Corresponding with the advance of the eye cover, her heart contracted and contracted with short expansion to feed the trying body. The heart pulled itself into an intense contracted mass of muscle where the fibers pulled and pressed down on one another, breaking and pulling apart. The implosion shot blood into every extremity; drenching the thirsty muscles and causing further downstream explosion of TLG's organs. Blood spouted through her digestive track where the pressure relief pulled the blood and pieces of flesh out of TLG's mouth. She dropped, crashing forward into the sand with her face half buried, her mouth dredging the sand as it slid with the momentum of the fall.

Soon, the path laid and marked many times as the creatures could not run any longer. The smaller beasts' remains were pushed aside as the larger and beast of all sizes continued to follow Vgi. Some of the remains of the fallen creatures were kicked, pushed into the stones that were apparently guarding the course, where the remains broke and bled. The flying creatures followed Vgi, trance-like, pushing and colliding in space, sometimes causing injury to others, damaging their ability to fly. Many of the larger and small flying creatures were knocked from the sky and trees. Some of the flying creatures survived the fall through the pocketed mass of moving land animals took up the trek on land. Others who survived the collisions in the sky were hit again by the creatures moving below, injured to the point of immobility where they died in the churn of the procession. Animal remains were crushed by the passing of the parade of the animals, fish, fowl and insects. The remains, mostly drained dry from over exertion, not showing any signs of the vaporous perspiration, and drool that the creatures experienced during the pursuit were now thin with taunt skins and furs of every color, texture and pattern laid across the many sets of motionless bones, gaped mouths, bared teeth and quiet peering eyes. Their lifeless hulls separated by stones, slight gusts of powdery blowing sand and the gathering of fallen tree twigs, branches and decaying leaves.

In the darkness, the beast turned ahead of Vgi. Now close enough, she saw the moon nearly full, spotted, bright and yellowish move along the surface of the beast's left eye as the beast turned, rolled back its eye to see Vgi and then quickly adjusted its vision forward into the dark night across the flat. Vgi was closing the distance between the two.

The hunting party trailed now in a carnival like state as the older hunters realized that no matter how the chase ended, that it was a glorious event. Vgi's father became less apprehensive as the days and nights of the chase passed. One evening in the flats, one of the fellow hunters approached Vgi's father and asked him to dance together as they ran and trailed Vgi.

The father, who would not make eye contact with the hunter, asked, "How can I dance? I may lose my daughter?"

The hunter's response, "You will lose your daughter" came out of the hunter's mouth with haste and a bit of cutting. He continued, "You may lose your daughter?" The hunter repeated back the father's words with sarcasm, but with a tone of plea to look at the situation differently.

"It might not be today, but it could be. You will lose her eventually, but now?" The hunter, still running, gestured to the activity occurring well ahead of them, "Her life will not be without the achievement and celebration...not ever!" The hunter engaged and spoke with a slightly raised voice and stern face of caring too much as their look at each other affirmed their knowing that this chase was one only a few adults come to make and overcome.

They moved on, bouncing along the flat. The father followed the hunter's gesture and no longer felt a sense of impending loss, but now saw Vgi's chase as a source of great pride no matter how it turned out. Their movements flowed into running dancing as they joined the carnival of the rest of the group. The hunters had long since abandoned the upper garment wraps in the chase and now moved barefooted with only minimal swaths of clothing with breasts, buttocks and backs exposed. They danced, ran, hugged, pressed cheek to cheek and sometimes turned to kiss each other's face in recognition and celebration of Vgi's performance up to this point.

They neared the flat's edge as the sky lightened. The beast turned ever so slightly as the dark morning sky phased into lighter shades of black, grey and blue. Vgi, getting closer, was on the young beast's right and trailing. The texture of the land beneath their strides was changing. It was like a half-healed scarred area of a great wound in the otherwise monolithic fabric. The smoothness now felt gritty, hard and bumpy. A minute later, the rocks, some jagged, some round and smooth, met their feet with every stride inflicting pain and damage. The beast caught the first glimpse of the rising sun; its curvature forming a small perfect arch over the horizon was portrayed and accounted for in the right dark eye of the beast by Vgi. They reflected on the same image as the beast turned again. It did not know the extent of the wound in the flat, but the beast plunged forward. The ground dropped off suddenly, and the beast dropped into empty space heading down to the boulders and jagged rocks below.

Vgi lost sight of the reflection of the sun; it dropped out of sight along with the rest of the silhouette of the beast. Vgi did not wait to reach that point in the wound on the land. She took a few more strides and pushed out of the rocks, up and out into the air. At the peak of her arc of travel in the air, she reestablished visual contact with the descending beast. They both moved downward now. As Vgi fell, she stretched out both arms over her head, spread her legs bent at the knees and arched her back. Her limbs felt the immediate relief of not running and began to become reenergized; her entire body relaxed. The high velocity air rushed onto, around and past her, contouring her skin and muscles. The beast, turning and out of control as it fell, saw Vgi, a dark underside, her back was slightly lit, hair flying; half dark, half lit with the coming sun flickered like a small fire in a light rain. She glided downward studying the beast for how she would kill it. As she passed beneath the lip of the wound, the faint sounds of the hunting party were no longer audible. Inside the wound, the darkness returned, and the sound of the passing air became more compressed. She knew they would hit soon.

Deeper in, Vgi could not see, but heard the beast hit. In attempt to survive, the beast withheld the screams of agony that accompany great injury, but the beast could not remain totally silent upon impact. Vgi detected the thud of the landing and the yelp of the beast and turned her body, altering the effects of the air on her body just enough to change her trajectory. Her eyes adjusted to the darkness, and she began to see that she had achieved what she needed to with the change in her downward path; she was heading right for the wounded and partially crushed beast. As she fell toward the beast, its dark eyes caught the light from the morning sky. The image sharpened with the approach, the light blue hues of the sky created a pale grey sheen in the beast's two orbs. The orbs' light cast just barely out and onto the creviced gashed sides of the wound. The shadowed protrusions and recesses filled Vgi's periphery as she stayed focused on the prey. The beast was more injured, but still alive and attempting to push along the boulders back to its feet to perhaps resume the chase, or finally turn on Vgi and destroy her with a single blow. Vgi adjusted her flying descent to match the movements of the beast and formed herself into an arriving deadly force. Vgi locked her right arm out ahead of her and turned, putting the first of her force behind the tips of her longest fingers on that hand. She did not calculate whether or not she would survive. It was not important then, but she instinctively aimed her leading hand at the beast's most vital organ. Just before impact and entering the body of the beast, the child, as best she could, released the hunting party word. This word was used in the administering of the conquering blow, the 'ku' or when the victory was at hand.

In the culture of her people, the word was delivered like a song. A word in note or over different notes depending on the situation. The word partially soaked into the walls of the wound and some of the song filtered out and was heard by the approaching hunting party.

They were pleased, but wondered if the young one had missed and used the word and "Was she really overcoming and safe?" they thought.

Vgi held the eye contact with the struggling beast, adjusting the aim of her forward hand inside of the miniscule final fractions of seconds. Her aim appeared true, pushing back and down on the beast's outer layer, bursting through its flesh and on to its hardened members. Still, Vgi's hand and arm made all the contact. Now her hand knifed deep into the beast. The beast released a deep, sorrowful, long moan as Vgi's word faded out. Vgi's fingers entered the beast's vital organ. The impact ruptured and detached it from most of the inner body. Her leading hand pushed against the beast's side against the rocks, her finger and hand bones crumbling. The force of the impact shot up her arm as the arm folded and snapped in several places. Vgi followed her arm, slamming into the body of the beast with her shoulder, head and chest. The internal bleeding that the beast had suffered under the pressure of Vgi's arrival shot out from where it was pooling, much of it sputtering out in globs from the beast's mouth and streaming out of its wounds and orifices where the blood comingled with bile and urine excrements. The full impact of her weight further crushed the bodily frame of the beast providing just enough resistance to prevent Vgi from being lost on the rocks.

"It would be the most hurtful loss," her father stopped refusing to feel the oncoming loss.

⁓

Vgi, in a seeming twist of fate, had gained favor and popularity among the Beings. Vgi was popular, capable and loved.

"Love for each other does not save us," her father said as he soured in seeing that Vgi was more admired for manly accomplishments than him.

The first to the edge, the father reached, covered with his opposite hand and checked his sheath and it appeared to be intact. He began his descent. Not picking, but careful, cliffside chess, his best game, steadied, stepped and met, foothold, toe, heel, hand, waist, weight, knee, nail and get. A spider, cloth draped, beard wet, back and over, high and low, he goes the Z pattern to Vgi and…

"What great force made this hole, popped marked, jagged edges with footholds, finger holes and knee cusp as virgin as candle light, but old as the forgotten," the father, gaining speed, negotiated the cliff to the sight of Vgi and her kill.

The others gathered about the edge, wondering as they followed the robes of the Father's side, cripplingly, contouring with nearly impossible stretches and feats of balance further across, up and down as the top of his forehead and hat, nape of his neck and backs of his legs, heels of his feet and swaying robes of cloth disappeared in the misty, dusty fog and darkness between them and Vgi.

Long since the time when he could have made a descent like Vgi just did and did what Vgi just did…the father made quick conclusions of the situation to see the squirming beast using its last energy to try to catch the fleeting air, every part of its existence in overdrive to survive. Vgi, having ricocheted off the beast, was just out of reach of the gnashing teeth and scratching claws, but close enough to be showered and soaked in the blood, vomit, excrement and saliva. He checked his sheath, moved toward Vgi, not sure of the words to say. The regret of her surpassing him in board games, witty comebacks, facts of history and physical displays of leadership bubbled up just behind the love for her survival. The calls from the others echoed down on them like the great song of a play, bouncing down and around the cliffs walls, some tracing the father's path, some faded in the fog, some sharp in the scratches on his arms and in the arm and side of her brittle mass. The mere vibration from their calls amplified the pain for Vgi and woke her to full recognition of the face that had always meant comfort and security, but this face was one she had never seen before. The father knew that the others could not see, but heard the grunts of the beast and knew that it was not yet dead.

"Funny how the vacuum of death, when it happens, fills the air and pushes the leaves, cheeks and solemn looks of beast to the same end."

"Forgive me."

"Still time for the kill and the credit."

The Father unchecked the sheath and drew his weapon. A flicker pierced the fog and dust and was blinked in the eyes of the others with slight pain. The unison because the shone, pressed stepped and toed showered pebbles, rocks and earth drift, the paths, and sounds of the cliffs. The slow-moving sky moved the clouds and pulsed with a small wind. As the father moved toward her, he moved into her view to the cliffs, limiting and sliding, right to left over the moonlight semi-vertical cuts across the father's pattern, the falling rocks, twigs outcrop from rocks, falling gathered shift of dirt and earth. Vgi could barely make out the others on the edge. Vgi could not make out their faces, but knew them from their colors, the curves of their cheeks, the gestures of their bodies and how they held the shoulders, necks, and heads. The father, remembering the days when he was great and not overshadowed by his daughter, drew down the weapon with still capable strength and aim.

Vgi thought of the moments when restraint may have been a better display than the mental and physical public and private dominance of the one with the weapon coming down. Wherever it landed, it was surely deserved.

RNi, of Vgi and for now, did not need to know more. With the parts of the words that were pronounced with an inhale making the most of the inhale and accomplishing all they needed to with the exhale, RNi seemed to get stronger with every breath. The muscles were working all over RNi's entire body. The muscles, seemingly without command, responded and acted just with the proper amount of push and pull to do whatever RNi thought for them to do. RNi rippled as a beautiful being and did not know how the Proven would conclude but was starting to believe that all of the training was more than adequate to compete to win.

"The Beings found it more difficult to catch the beasts and would find it more difficult to protect themselves and to prevail during times of conflict."

The distant spectators, who could only get so close to the course of the Proven, assessed RNi as they did with all the participants, but they did not hear RNi's song.

—for Us—

The Commander, beginning to feel the coming desperateness of the military situation, decided to forget his pride for the time being and acquiesced to the need for him to inform the council back home of the impending trouble with the now cloudy battle.

"Look," the Commander turned to Compranellosis, the Commander's Aide, "I shall not ever again gaze upon the living faces of so many of my fallen Sons."

Compranellosis responded, "You are in command, the minds and hearts of the enemy commanders, soldiers, slaves, and deities quibble with uncertainty. The day is long and long from decided against us."

"If the day is decided against us here, the nation must go on. We must quickly get information to the capital and to the council so that the people can be informed about the potential harm that may be approaching soon. I have prepared this message that is to be delivered as quickly as possible."

'Sir, the last horses were eaten last night."

"The distance is great, but must be traversed, as every minute that we can give them to prepare may save the lives of hundreds of our people. Our children will not be raped and enslaved by their marauding soldiers. Our wives and daughters will not be taken as possessions used in every way to cater and to please their leadership. Our fathers and brothers will not be tortured and put to death in the most gruesome and undignified means, likely to be used by our dastard enemy."

The Commander thought without saying, for this, too, took too much time; his face said it all. He looked like a totally different person now that he was consumed with the realization of being defeated; his comrades and brothers in arms lost to the sword, axe, hammer, spear, stone and bow. He knew that before the next morning, he would be executed while his conqueror stared him down.

Compranellosis motioned the other men into the presence of the Commander and turned to announce the Soldier, "Sir, this is VGR, the messenger. VGR will trek back carrying your instructions to the council for the survival of our people."

The opposing Army, across the entire breadth of the lines, small fighting groups and horse mounted contest, clashing groups, moved-in, began to appear, having bloodily fought their way at the crest of hills, surmounting cliffs, before trees, seizing more and more of the field. The Commander's Army, to a man to ensure survival, contracted and contracted closer and closer. They closed in search of the comfort and protection of their fellow soldiers. The opposing Army carefully and steadily moved to squeeze the Commander's Army whose soldiers fell in small scores or one by one as if to melt into the ground on which they laid. Their faces held lifeless indifference accented with the figures of last thoughts, sorrows, regrets and their consciousness gave way to injury or pain as they faded away from the physical world, yet peace of no longer wondering which battle would be the battle to end their lives.

...dampened old clothes, sprinkling, drizzling, sprinkling, drizzling, mold in the light of sunny then cloudy day..."

The Commander gave what he knew would be the last signature scrolled with the normal rhythm of his hand, jagged, almost trembling, yet smoothly certain. The movements, VGR stood feeling like he was in another world, intently followed with his eyes, shifting, chasing, adjusting just behind the hand, wrist, arm and pin. The singular line flowed, curved, turned, jumped, pointed and flowed again, trailing off in a final sweeping strike. VGR slightly turned his head to follow the sweeping strike as it appeared to approach the edge as it disappeared; the Commander's stance, armor and motion turning with the sweep, blocked VGR's view. VGR turned his head with the sweeping motion, and his attention was further pulled in the direction of the sweep, far out in the distance where the clash of the victors brought more men down seemingly by the hundreds, pounding the earth like a drum. VGR saw the war continue on its course, closer and closer to the army command field palace. VGR, feeling spared at least for now, thought how the defeated show much more bravery and honor than the victors.

The Commander completed enough of the turn, scrolled the message with one hand and reached and grasped a message seal container. The Commander lowered the scrolled message, releasing some of the hand pressure, allowing the scroll to unwind a bit and to fit snuggly in the seal container. The Commander capped the container, applied his seal, continued on the turn, a passing gaze out to the war that remained still very active, yet decided. The Commander completed the turn to face VGR. They exchanged a brief stare to know that they will never see each other again. VGR, knowing that the guard, being attentive, but also aware of the pending ever more encroaching doom as the smell of fresh blood and bile seeped into the palace from the field, loved the Commander and would do all to protect him.

"This has to be done," VGR thought as he reached to meet the Commander's presentation of the sealed message container.

The Commander's signature seemed to be right with the world, but his presentation of the container was totally different. The Commander was right-handed, but extended with his left hand to give the container to VGR.

"Forgive me," VGR said as he grasped the message container with his left hand and in the same moment, drew a minor sword.

The guards re-calibrated on VGR and moved in weapons first toward VGR. They would have him in milliseconds.

"Could he be a spy or a traitor?" the Commander thought in that instance. "I have known VGR's family all of my life. Either would be more impossible than the raging war."

"Wait," the Commander said in a mixed tone of a plea and an order with such force and sincerity that the nearing engagements caught it in their ears and thought at how it could be for them, but it was not.

"This is...," VGR couldn't finish the sentence, and the Commander knew that he didn't have to finish it.

The guards held their distance, slightly confused. Should they save the Commander or obey him?

Unlike any message, this message, every word and its purpose maybe never heard of or spoken of for the rest of time, enters the annals of a plight, of a people, of a country and of an idea.

VGR and the Commander, in a brief gaze of finality, acquiesced to what had to be done. VGR raised the short sword to the extent of his reach as the guards, held motionless by the mystical interaction between VGR and the Commander, witnessed. VRG, in a ceremonial turn of the sword and movement of his arm, glided the razor cutting-edge of the sword down onto the Commander, grazing his forehead, across his face, skipping his neck, over the frontal part of his right shoulder, out, around, down and across his abdominal armor marking the surface with the traces of blood. VGR, with the same rapidity and smooth motion, creased the inner left arm and then down across the upper left leg. It, the blood under the command of the evolutionary bounds, adorned the Commander in stripes, loops, curls and runs.

They all, realizing the shortness of time, felt the finality and the meaning of the act as the war pressed closer to the palace. VGR, with a similar style of movement almost in reverse order, waved the message container over the Commander's wounds and bleeding, covering the seal, historical markings, handling scratches, tie lines and hand-held wear indentions.

" ...Commander crimson..."

Without another word, VGR, with short sword in one hand and the message container in other, walked toward and past the Commander, brushing shoulder to shoulder as he passed, through the still, motionless guards and out toward the way home.

The Commander, in an almost trance-like state, donned his head peace.

"They will know...," he thought. He no longer had to think, but in his deepest being humored in knowing the enemy army, in search of, having been told and taught, was, of course, way off course from the true prize and headed in the wrong direction.

He began a steadfast walk toward the encroaching war as most of the guards followed. The few others held motionless by their fears, thoughts of home, their mates, children and the survival instinct telling them that if they stayed somehow, they would survive. Some wanting to go with VGR and some just not able to face the moment stood and watched the palace become empty of its sense of power, its sense of control and its sense of existence.

VGR and FTLY were born and raised by the same groups. As they were meant to and often did and nearly nightly did, the elder women intermixed with the younger and within the crying distance of the scurrying playing children, but nearly out of sight. The central camp fire rippled, sparked, whipped, flamed up and receded. So many stratifications of beauty, the dull eyed eternity, the bright blues, the coal colds, the patterned dress and flesh, fire light and night sky. The meditation and rhythm only appreciated by a few and VGR, as the women shared the news, the rumors, exaltations, and condemnations of others in their chats, whispers, and announcements.

VGR's song played in his head and the thought to sing, but he did not. While growing up, VGR and with the many fires, VGR could run and play and match his jumps, steps, falls and words with the development of the fires depending on when extra logs were added, the coals stirred and so on. The few women noticed VGR and knew his future. The women remembered FTLY and kept a special ear out for his roaming about with the other young ones. It was often recounted around the fires of the night that FTLY was born making fists, with grimace. FTLY would be a soldier, VGR, the Order.

As the Commander and the band of guards began to engage the massive swarm, horse, chariot, arrows, axe, and shields, VGR, FLTY and one of the guards joined in more than eye contact, but gave a look that retraced their very different lives and how they had come to these places where they now stood. VGR wanted to save FTLY, FLTY knowing that he could not go and could not last if he went; his defeated countenance purposefully told VGR, "Leave me to die."

The horse meat in his stomach would soon be fed to the enemy's dogs.

VGR walked to go outside of the palace. The last remains, papers, seals, decanters, sheaths, sheets and sets of the Commander, just now so ordered, now mysteriously suddenly strewn about. Once outside, VGR lifted his walk to a solemn trot. Once at speed, horse could not outlast him, and the chariot could not follow him through the rugged paths and mountainous inclines, turns, and crevices. He began to feel safe and notched up his pace.

VGR could hear the fading, metal to metal and the now lesser thuds of men hitting the earth, sounds of the war as he extended his distance more and more from the palace. He heard the seemingly last violent throng of a war that held the span of a hundred miles echo across the back of his neck and past the face and out against the approaching hills. VGR, knowing that the first priority was to get the message back to the people, felt for the Commander, the guards; the men and began to cry. VGR gathered the thoughts and remembered how precious the tears were and having sheathed the short sword, began to wipe the tears into the mouth to prescrve the water level. The sounds of the war faded and faded to become more and more faint as VGR's body adjusted to top distance speed.

The hills, paths, mountains, rocks, trees, shrubs, weeds, insects, beasts and birds...the hills, paths, mountains, rocks, trees, shrubs, weeds, insects, beasts and birds, each flashed in and out of his con-sciousness as the earth passed between his toes with each stride and take.

"Once touched, a heart pearl bares, scares, and tears in like a little baby curls away from our world of sin."

VGR, not quite audibly, reviewed the cadence and the words into his running rhythm. VGR's running hand motion moves the message container in and out of his view as he strides along, the Commander's blood drying into place as if meant to complete the decor of the message container. VGR continued to move and move more toward the transcendent state.

VGR knew and showed with the relaxed muscles on his face and calmness in his eyes, "This is what will take me home." The ultimate purpose of his life.

VGR's memory and consciousness flashed to the materials, colors, textures and the many varying contact and movement sounds of the uniforms of the Commander, the guards and the Army and flashed to memories of the mate that surely waited and worried.

"Back to warm darkness and no squint my princess, my African princess, the light is meant."

The mate, surely worried, "How does one person withstand the burden to worry for over 200,0000 lives?" VGR contemplated the struggle the people must have had in worrying about the Army, the war, the outcome and what was to come afterwards.

"A little longer then soon," VGR thought. "You, for one, for one my love, will know."

The unknown is actually a mystery and not an existence, object or fact waiting to be discovered.

"The people are dealing with so much mystery. Soon, you will know as well. The Army has heroically faced, fought and delayed an overwhelming force to provide time for our people to make preparations to ensure the survival of our culture, history and way of life.

VGR paced himself with the elements of the night taking in all the cues from the stars and moon washed sand, nightscape, and the obliviousness beyond his sight. VGR did not lose his connection and cadence with the words.

"I wait and take, like the Black Volta, slow so much and think."

VGR crossed the rising sun and turned into more bareness devoid of any sign of the human endeavors.

"... that force us across these lands," VGR thought. "It wasn't long ago, the Army heading in the opposite direction, traveled through this very route, on the way to face the enemies.

VGR recalled the dutiful, but happy faces of the fresh soldiers, not marching, not racing, not running, but moving at a speedy pace and how the Seniors, despite their best efforts, could not totally get the look of seriousness and determination of their faces and in their gaze. The mid-agers faces were emotionless, but their words and commands were exacting with balanced punch for effect. The new ones and the young, freshly dressed, at first struggled to keep the pace, sometimes jeering and gesturing with their buddies, quickly get in shape after a few days of being on the move. VGR thought back to the soldiers once smiling with a sense of adventure, falling to their deaths in broad swaths of waste.

"She runs, runs away, beats it, heavy and faint, so far, look back, but forget or outlast love, heart pearl, can't, can't, can't."

VGR flashes back to the mate, the family and the people. VGR blinked the dawn from his thoughts and transcendence from dominance in his mind. The day, evening and night from the war has put much distance on his body as it pushed, pulled, stretched and contracted every muscle, organ and bone to go farther and farther and closer and closer to home. VGR's hair has long since been drenched and matted with sweat, night dew, rain and foggy mist.

Not the face, the mate, but the grace, are VGR's thoughts as he senses to near the wilderness of the time of youth and the adventures of trips with friends. VGR replays the grace and the innocence of the children, slowing down the recollections to be more at pace with the gallop. Intermixed with the war recollections, VGR recounts the bright day's sun and the clouds when leaving the palace, the dust from the war, breathed in deep while setting out, and how the air cleared while approaching the foothills and even clearer while increasing the elevation passing through the lower hills and eventually the mountain's passes in the frigid air within an arrow shot or the distance of the mate's smile, VGR warmed to the smile of the peaks. The grace, the simple routine adorned, accented in some many ways. Some with color, fragrance and that feeling in hand, the body against the inner arm, face touching face, grace trusting pace.

VGR, in an inadvertent swing, brushes his arm against the message container in the carrying pouch and involuntarily increases the velocity pushing the body beyond the limits of performance known before.

With the totality of the lengths, breaths and depths of all of VGR's inhales and exhales, VGR's jumping gazes focusing, refocusing on near-scapes and far-scapes, and far long stares. The lengths of the forward and backward swings of both arms, hands and finger tips, VGR felt the immensity and the finality beginning to emerge, slowly spreading, coating, floating over the lining of the inner body and inner limbs; moving under the skin and permeating outward to the surface and around VGR's being.

The remains and evidence of the outskirts of existence began to pass more and more when VGR chose to take account. The slightly grown over hunting trails, curls, snake crawls disappear in the brush, trees and darkened canopies. The broken tools and weapons lay discarded in the grass, dirt, weeds and graves. VGR's path, familiar, the places once played, the cuts and scrapes, hills behind lakes and the strolls, first dates, the fights and kites, berries, fruits and likes, approaches farmers' fields, antique shields, animals, back to palace pieces strewn, the walls of the city so far from the Marathon.

—Chasity Zoo—

The maggots toiled in the muddy paths, not certain, but not so much guessing about the encounter. The rain finished, and soaked trees pushed with the breeze, rising vapors off the land and trees, to the maggots' left. Recoiling back with the contraction of the breeze, the overlapping leaves, before they dripped, held mirror-like the thin layer of water on each stem, twig and leaf caught and magnified the brilliant facial profile, half tree height of the observing Keeper. The breeze washed away the reflective water and pushed the leaves and trees back to the left. Contracting again, the Keeper met the maggots, one regal, the others nearly destitute.

The Keeper in the reverence emanating from the gathered candidates did not walk, strut, stride or run, but moved to begin, and the Keeper did recite some of the keys of history and hopes for the future. The Keeper seemed to roll out accounts, actions and facts of history from pure memory without notes or cues of any kind. Some of the notes were more readily understood as an isolated piece of information, and others understood to connect to the interconnected causes and effects of events covered in the other sessions or in the Keepers' presentations.

The Keeper continued, " How far back would you like to go?" Anticipating silence and inaction, the silence and inaction that is guaranteed when the relationship between teacher and pupil is without sustainable challenge.

"Let's go," the Keeper, after pause, began. "Let's start at the end, the end that does not exist. It does not exist," he added for emphasis.

"We will get back to that."

The Keeper jumped back to another area, now posing questions to tell the story.

"There has been great difficulty in remembering to ask simple questions. For example, with the 'The Three Kings' in their kingdoms, were there artisans, craftsmen, buildings, artists, ones of letters, medicine and so forth? Probably, I am sure that you will agree. Why three, why those three? What if the crowns of the three were made to be three pieces of an interlocking single crown jewel composition for the highest. Have you thought about crown design? The Order?"

"Let's move forward. The INs (the controlling ones) outlawed sex to stop the spreading of diseases that ravaged the world and threatened extinction. Sex was controlled and practiced only in laboratory theater settings. Most procreation was manufactured. Sex was no longer allowed. The INs determined that the natural interchange of bodily contact and the 'gross' passing of bodily substances from one to another had to be checked. It was the only way to save the species. The people would not control it, the INs rationalized."

"Even in the face of the damaging, deadly proof that sex, the most selfish of all endeavors of the species, seeded and was fundamental to the development of all cancers, they would not stop it, even to save themselves or their others or heirs.

All were correct to be concerned, but only so correct. Like with most problems, the answer is predicated on something simple that for a variety of reasons was not able to be realized. To preserve the race, there are a couple of simple, presently unexplored options. The idea is of course lifted as it were from the early civilizations; portrayals like the minotaur, winged Isis or Pegasus and now the mascots of your favorite teams. It is the fantastic capabilities that we believe to find in the joining of the strengths of different beings, real or mystical.

"The point is the combi...," the Keeper broke the full pronunciation. The Keeper took account of the bewilderment on their faces.

"What am I wasting my time with you for?"

—Mind Cycles—

"Do you want to study or jump around from thought to thought? The capacity for concentration is directly related to the purity level of the blood and the intensity of the actions and intents. The rhythm of thought is a sporadic cadence seldom controlled or slowed down or sped up. The thinking jumps from subject to subject with brief analyticals and depths. Material that attempts to meld thought into a concentrated monastic path of energy runs contrary to the natural rhythm. Material that supports the natural rhythm amplifies the natural occurrence enhancing the thought process and making it better, more efficient and thus superior."

Mki thought, "We are all brilliant."

Mki opened all means of information available and saw the main hints, clues, and tracings of some of the historically brilliant of the species.

Mki pondered where to begin, "The ancients of Asia, Africa, Greece, Rome would not do."

She determined that the greatest find, the best example, would not be one wrapped in the power structures or commissioned like a Da Vinci.

"Someone existed."

"Someone like her that knew, knew perhaps about the Order or perhaps knew about why the Order was a part of us."

"Who would it be?"

⚘

The dry period of 1910 was challenged and in some ways overcome by simply collecting the water as it fell to the surface. The soil collects the water, the waters collect the water, the plants collect the water. Now it was obvious, its clearness applies to no kind of color. When pure it is tasteless and odorless, it's part of everything. The water replenishes, over replenishes and then destroys. The weight of the ocean and its miles and miles and tonnage and tonnage and immeasurable pressures could not crumble the core.

AQi woke surprisingly refreshed. Her nude body moved out of the covers, and the air began to envelop her, rolling over and pressing onto her skin, seeping into her pores, sweeping along the trunks of her billions of hair follicles from the back of her neck to the back of her calves, the air fitted around and joined her. All at once, the air pushed in, tugging at the particulate matter attached to the fibers. The new air rolled in with the force of the ocean and the glide of the tide reacquainting with AQi. She was cool as she thought about the comfort she felt while at rest under the covers and the slight push she felt from the cool air and its morning.

"Why do I sleep nude?" AQi thought as she moved to make ready for the day.

Even if I slept with clothing, the morning would still be felt upon me.

AQi reflected back to different times in her life when she remained awake all night and for days for various reasons. Whether it was the work, her studies, her hobbies or with her lovers, it did not matter now.

"The morning always comes," she remembered the rough transla-
tion of the quote from the Worshipping Times.

"Yes, the morning comes, but it comes with a purpose and meaning.
Each morning is different with different messages and the same message"

"Today, you should move along the path toward tomorrow with invigoration."

"That's it," she thought as she lowered herself down to release her
urine. It streamed out and away from her. AQi rose and moved to the
water supply. She needed it. It refilled her. She listened reassuringly as
the water cleaned her and she stood ready for the next encounter.

Her stride was short and heavy as she moved through the room,
she thought, "That only took about ten minutes."

"She reflected at times it takes longer, at times it takes shorter."

As AQi moved, her partner, from the sound of it, was stirring. The
shower was running, the droplets bounced and sprayed seemingly to
barely touch her cheek, forearm and the spot on her foot just behind
the pinky toe along the skin back toward the ankle.

She did not even think but realized in that billi-second of time,
"The wet sensation was too pronounced for its scale."

Audibly different than the roar of the shower, the outer door
clicked shut, self-locking with a back-to-back, but distinctly separate
mechanical click after closing, affirming that he left. AQi saved any outward expression for lack of an audience. She caught a glimpse of her
facial posture and body language in the reflection of the smaller circular
hand mirror that had been opened, readied and positioned, just there
nearly a month ago. Yeah, it was adjusted slightly a little while cleaning
and what not, but it did not move and there it was.

Inside of the next second, AQi stepped into the waters, reached to
drench her face and to lather her hands as she revisited the brief image
in the small mirror. Her tranquil facial profile, relaxed jaw skin, raised

brow not contemplative nor falsely happy, slightly masked around the ear, outer-eye and back of the neck by the veil of parsed strands of head hair coming together at the front of the opposite shoulder, bouncing as she moved, laying down along the outward and upward curve of her breast. She could not see the ear fully, but it was there. The ear pushed out beneath the strands showing its impression in the flow. It wasn't reflex, it wasn't habit. It must have been natural for AQi to lift her corresponding hand. She moved nearly out of the grasp of the reflection toward the drawing sound of the shower stream and almost jerkily, but gracefully, pulled her loose hair back together and seated it behind her ear revealing the full exposure of her thin, naked and delicate ear not scratched, no markings, no piercing, no discoloration.

"Did the tips of her head hair, nearly invisible to the naked eye, ever so slightly reach and touch her breast nipple area?" She did not notice that sensation before.

She knew what she felt then, the facial profile hinted to a face full with satisfaction. In the mirror, the remainder of her body was equally relaxed in knowing that he left like he did, bested in every way. AQi smiled inside and submerged herself in the steady stream of refreshingly warm shower water. This was different again, out of the covers, the air and moisture took her over into the water. She is covered again. Smiling largely caused a rush of energy to radiate out from her core to the rest of her body. It felt like a stretch without moving a muscle. Inside, the energy sensation burst through whatever means of travel it had, all through her body and into the tiny crevices of her inner flesh first igniting her entire back. It splashed on the backs of her upper arms and legs, more in the frontal thigh. The fleshy muscles responding with slight trembles as the wave passed. AQi pushed out a deep inhale releasing pressure on her upper body. The sensation flowed down, relaxing the calves and forearms, dancing and then fizzing out in the toes, fingers and scalp. Outside, the waters ran down over her like forever complimenting the physical inside effects. It all became audible as she did not wish nor could she contain it any longer. The sounds she made were out of her control. AQi made the sounds, but did not have any influence in the decisions of the sound's tone or duration. It came and went as the feeling rescinded.

AQi thought, "What would he have thought about the sounds if he was still here?"

"If he was still here, the sounds would have been different."

The sounds she did make worked with the feelings she was experiencing. She closed her eyes and let the sounds permeate her being, following the paths of the smile's energy throughout her body, but at the same time closing out the rest of her sound world. AQi chose not to hear anything else. Within ten feet of her, the sounds of the motion of touching and moving objects, the watches, the clocks, the functioning micro-bio-mechanisms of her world were ignored. Still further, her entertainment and appliance-home support and machines, computers calculating on command and within their automated processes made sounds were phased out. Outside, the world whirled on, oblivious to AQi now with billions upon billions of engagements and activities within her ear shot, but she had chosen and heard only herself and the water. She was able to hone into the flow, discerning the sounds of the flow on her back from the sounds of water swishing through her body hairs. As the sounds amplified in succession and in unison, her focus went deeper with the flow, spray, the falling water, and the waves along the shower floor. Her hairs rippled like a flown damp flag in the gusty wind. The hair stems bending, and hair ends popping as the flow pushed and pulled them about. AQi dialed into the unison whipping and popping of billions of her hair ends in the glistening flow. The resultant sound to the dialed in ear was like shotgun blasts, but each explosion seemed to be a massage to AQi's fine muscular frame. AQi focused deeper as she found the experience very pleasing with solace, relief and relaxation. She opened her eyes, but nothing registered in her vision but a brightness. The sounds sparked, cracked, softly exploded and moved, resonating down from her inner ear, transmitted from bone to flesh to bone again throughout her body. AQi was not able to fully control herself as her physical body gently collapsed in the shower. AQi rolled over her legs on to the shower floor, consumed by the infinite changes and continuity of sounds of the flow as she fell. In an instant, she was consumed inside and out. "The unanimity," she thought, "the unanimity,"…she thought to herself. "My God," she did not need to say or do anything else… "Why was something different this time?"

AQi thought about her mate who left just moments earlier, "He may as well have left. Any conversation with him would have reached the same conclusion." She never felt alone in the shower. She focuses. Afterward, she felt new.

"Boy," she thought "that only took about ten minutes also."

Stepping out with the eyes closed, she cleared her face and brow, the entirety of her naked body still glistening with the showers remains. AQi began to pamper herself, starting to dry her toes, feet and legs. She examined her parts and reviewed their condition, fitness and changes since her last washing; every inch, none untouched. Once while passing the towel over her shin, AQi noticed a pigmented spot just below her right calf. This morning, the freckle was still there. The reddish-brown freckle's irregular circular shape blended nicely with the irregular curves of her leg. The reddish-brown color complemented the pinkish and off-white of her skin. With the pinky finger of her right hand extended out, AQi contorted her bent body around, giving herself a view of the freckle. It was the color of her breast nipples. Her pinky contacted the spot, and AQi noticed that the texture was of nipple texture as well. The nipple she knew, but the spot caused her to wonder.

She pressed the towel more firmly against her skin and down to where the follicles laid drenched many times over from the inundating water from the shower. One by one, many by many, thousands by thousands, her hand pushed in on the towel, sweeping up her legs. She exfoliated, losing hairs, old skin and fraying surfaces of the pigmented areas as she goes. She feels different. As the towel passes quickly along its path, the refreshing air again, moist, light, tingly and bonding with her passes over skin. AQi could feel the difference. The harmony passed not only through her mind, but her realization. This was now part of her being, and she knew that her being was a little different now. This part of her being and knowing was much different than a fact or piece of information that can be dumb spoken, shared, recited without meaning for participation in the communication, conversation, or media; like the type of communication that was the way of most individuals. Most individuals use the casual repetitious sounding of facts and the summation of events as history.

AQi thought about her being now, "Others will know. Only the ones who know or know similar things will know. The others that do not know will not notice."

Upon realizing this, AQi made it pass her reflection, almost afraid that she might not have changed. She reached, extending the right arm beyond the elbow, raising the upper arm just enough to ensure the reach was adequate. Without thinking, she moved to take care of her mouth as the waters readied. Her right hand began the water and she moved her left hand up near the top of her hip, her forefinger and thumb spread just to the point of stretching strain and cusped her hip along the buttocks. AQi caressed herself with deliberate steady movement, letting the web of her hand bowl over the follicles. Still freshening from the new air, the web brushed the skin with a sensation. AQi completed the step by slightly closing the cusp of her hand until the thumb pressed through her skin hair, impressing upon the skin of her upper buttocks. The remaining fingers spread along, traveling up the frontal thigh and resting on her flat boney front hip pelvis spot. In the millisecond that her fingers, web, palms and hand passed over her hip and thigh, AQi felt the sensation as different.

"Why?" she thought, "was her own touch new?"

The waters ran and she could not make out audibly what was happening outside of a few feet away. She noticed the solitude. She glanced back to where she expelled, then down. When she looked up, she knew that she knew something. She did not know or care if it was profound or not, but knowing this made her a little different. AQi knew that this part of her being was not a fact. It was an integral part of her being. It would be part of everything that she would think, be, know and do for the remainder of her existence.

"Hope this is a long time," she thought to herself, as the water, now completely gone.

AQi sees in the mirror the water color of her eyes. The color of the eyes and the color of the sky indicates a timing of influence and power for individuals.

The unique brown skin was a perfect match with the soil of inner North America. The American slave trade was foretold by the gravity and destiny pulling the Negro to its rightful place. Once there, it was only a matter of time before destiny began to pull on the outcomes of history. (The future must be a dark mist but edged in light). The English and Asian lands on the shore and the Nordics in the snowy icy cold. The Arabs, whose skin color contains ranges of sandy hues, contained enormous harmony with the land, so it was no mystery that the land would give back a thousand times for their devotions, commitments, and sacrifices.

The first thing, the repetitious coming of the morning, the sensation of the light and air. The promise of something new, something different, something better than before.

It began to come clear to AQi, "If there was meaning and purpose in one thing, one thing so simple, so obvious, so pervasive…"

AQi knew today was the last day that she would live in the time of not knowing.

—The Core (Brown Skin)—

Mki's first lesson was to understand the phases of existing. There was no ceremony. The acts of knowing were without unnecessary gestures of place, recognition of authority and acknowledgements of the unknowing to the knowing. Mki came to know how some small parts of existence will be ordered. Now her understanding would be completed.

The 'Z' pattern of time. Time is not always a linear measurement. We do not always move in a linear fashion to promote forward momentum or progress. Individuals, groups, societies, countries, empires exist from morning to morning. Each morning can and edge forward along the continuum or back. Back in the same direction or skewed at angle with the previous direction. When this pattern of movement is repeated, the traces of the individual experiences form a 'Z' like pattern and a double arrow like pattern, but the pattern is a measurement of the events as compared to the events of the past of the future. Progress in time is only progress when the criteria in which we judge the past and the criteria that we judge the present and the future share comparable value. The value need not be equal because if the value is equal, then there is no difference in the past, present, and future in terms of time and experience. Therefore, to affirm time and the progress of experience, we must change our judgements and values else we hinder our own development and we do and still might.

—Passion Bombs Away—

They came to the place where the carnal energies flowed. The INs knew nothing about the spots. Some of the spots were surface spots, some were sub-surface, some were 'aerials.' In the past, explorers at first considered a silly cult began to seek the spots through wandering and reporting. The Wanderers, or Ones as they came to be called, used techniques, used maps and used navigational tools, crude for that time. They wanted everyone to be able to interpret the maps and benefit from the spots' various energy forms.

◈

"This part of life is good too," Pl, almost questioning the committee, supplanting the answer to agree with her statement.

Pl was one who had made her way through life by being very practical. She had experienced a fairly routine up-bringing and tended to not be too swayed by major events of her times. The events did not seem to impact her or ones in her immediate surroundings to a significant degree. She had always kind of done the things that society said that she was supposed to do and up until the recent times, life was proceeding as she expected. Since she began volunteering with community groups, people noticed her abilities to reason with others and to reduce conflict where, surprisingly, all sides usually came away feeling satisfied.

The INs, who usually made very sound decisions about leading their society, made the proclamations to outlaw sex. The community members asked Pl to be their spokesperson.

"Even when it is not for contributing to the continuation of the Species, it is indeed contributing," Pl stated.

While presenting herself as a personal example of overall fitness through exercise of her limbs as well as her breast, buttocks, legs, arms, hands, feet and pubis, a breeze seeped in as she concluded her remarks, pushing her garments against her flesh and forming a single line from the tip of her raised hand's outside finger. The line continued down the outward curve of the outer fleshy part of her hand continuing smoothly over the wrist; without interruption as Pl paused in stance, the line with increasing speed, glided over the longer rises of her outer arm joining with the garment just past the shoulder. The line became blurred along the broadness of her back muscles with a slight lobe round the outer breast then relenting to the contraction of the waist.

Pl turned and rotated with the rhythm of the wind to further bring her point home and to ensure the audience of the other side of the room received the same information.

The line abruptly, yet with necessity, sharply made the buttocks turn and then rejoined the lazy, firm lines of the upper thigh. The line hesitated over the outer knee and continued along the vertical cliffs of her lower legs, gathering at her ankles and feet and starting back up again.

"Our bodies must be exercised to remain completely fit. If we allow one part of our bodies to be mal-used or atrophied, it will surely impact the whole," Pl concluded.

The second argument was made by one of the INs. Her name was Nv. Nv was one of the best educated women in their society. She was just past being a young adult. Her upbringing was nothing close to normal. Her family wrought out and maintained prominence and success. They and she were part of the superlatives of the society. Nv's parents were INs, and she agreed and felt obligated to uphold what the INs were proposing. She was equally as striking as Pl, but her eyes held refinement and scholarship where Pl's held the deepness of honesty and the remnants of pain of trial and error.

"We can protect everyone and still preserve the species by adopting these measures," Nv led with her conclusion.

"I don't need to have sex." She paused to let everyone look and to know that she was still without the experience and that she was fine.

"I do hope to one day have a family and with these measures, I am assured that I can have a family without fear of being hurt by one of these diseases. These diseases are killing us. The population is already at an uncontrollable and unsupportable level. We, as a society, expend great amounts of resources, large proportions of our individual and collective wealth to protect us from ourselves. It is a sad reality, but something has to be done. I believe that this will help."

Midway through, the audience, one of the participants, turned to a friend and said, "She does know what it is like to have a true mate?"

The participant's words seemed to come just as Nv was concluding her remarks.

"They would not control it," the INs rationalized.

Even in the face of the damaging deadly proof that sex, the most selfish of all endeavors of the species, seeded and was fundamental to the development of all cancers, they would not stop it even to save themselves or their others.

The members participated in the IN's process, supplanting and cheating the intricate supporting processes that were intended to ensure compliance or adherence. The Order would not comply or adhere. The Order knew, and knowing changed the equation by which the Process was established.

—Undeniable—

Forest, Part II

No warning, rain, a single drop, pierces the air, streaking furls, trail, sphere, hurls thru space, head-on they select, pop connects, splatters, roars, pours, pours, pours and drowning microbes and insects.

Moist soft path, trampled in, sin, defecating spot, hooved, whores, heat, sweet, wild and lots, remains, life, death indifference.

Steps record, flea, foul, beast, carnivore, awash, quenched, flinching teeth protracts, mud and dust, the moon turns, watches, joy disgust.

Suffocates, spreads, cake icing the goo, gasp after gasp after gasp, past, rolls, eternal howls harmony, agony last.

❧

Bl sat, and they sat. Her face, before strode and tense, now fallen, convinced in an inevitability. Her eyes, large, round and perfect to the lash, held the gaze of anticipation, emancipation, anticipation, captivation last.

"Out there," she brought back to her forethought.

"Out there, they wait."

"Wait," she said to herself.

"Wait," she said inaudible to them because she sat in the ready room just before her performance, feat, obligation.

Bl continued, knowing, reflecting to once when she rose way too soon and engaged. Waiting, naturally now, she did not care or dare to worry....

"About what, schedule?"

She turned and inspected her nails, pearls, frills and every detail.

"It's coming," her skin first and then her hand began to absorb the will, the undeniable compel to go and give.

Bl did not resist, but let it come into her, pass her skin. She slowly closed her eyes so that the lids would be surprised. It streamed in, again and again and again, relent, relent and relent she crossed the ready room floor. The passage did not matter and nor did they that lingered there. Bl noticed, but did not notice, striding, pride about to display. It, the feeling and weight of providing for so many, fell upon her as did the chance to provide for so many. Bl strode as she approached the focal point of the feat. Her garments, with hesitancy, blew back, black and trailed the front part of her toes, ankles, shins, knees, thighs, abdomen, breast, shoulders, face and head. As they blew back, the garments silhouetted her mature body in the light as she continued her procession. It dug and dug into her familiar, she gained, it gained on the way to them.

She knew not to think, but to remember and she did. Her gaze could not encompass the immense space, so she scanned without moving her head or eyes. Bl absorbed the complete presence, the complete presence of every fellow, fawn and dawn to come. The garments relaxed and swayed back in drape with a little perspiration.

Bl's legs became non-existent; the rest of her abdomen seeped sweat. Her face, stonily relaxed, consigned to embrace before the race, took in the thousands there and the millions more that were not. She gusts into the center abruptly pausing to wait on the last bit. Bl directly cast down, out, up and over and away the chance to escape.

"You are Bl's", she murmured in her head, arms out and upwardly stretched.

"You are..." she could not repel the coming yell any longer. Bl, of course, was beautiful in every way.

The crown of Bl's head produced the most graceful crest in the flow of her thick, color rich hair that cascaded about her face. Her face was beyond expression and even further from words. A thousand ships, Medusa lips, cheeks like hips, not too this, not too that...perfect fat, precious cat, lash, ear, a blank eternal stare. Her face did not speak, but remained humbled in talent honed in the many hours, days, and years in the many practices of expression, solving, knowing, caring, believing sacrificing, dedicating and loving impeccable traces of fury, jubilation, worry, contemplation, pleasure and indifference rounded out her facial demeanor. The unreal accents of blush, skin-stick, powder blended again perfection on perfection. Her mouth easy without tenseness, lips barely parted, covered in countless layers of the most unusual unique color. (The colored became known as Song). They recognized to never have seen it before and were awed.

The incalculable wide spreading lines of her lips alone were enough to tame the clouds to her will. Endless, co-mingling, redoubling with increasing calming intensity and yet she did not begin. The lower portions of Bl's face, in perfect symmetry, connected to the absolutely portioned neck on the verge of being muscular, gentle, beginning and ending like the life of a new born precious, coal black baby. Its line continued over and around Bl's shoulders. The garments would not hide, but glide again spread, raised, just above the surface aligned and preserved obvious power. They were the reason for human's dominion over the living world. Bl's arms continued the image and impact of the shoulders pinnacling through the main parts of her hand and fingers. Slight, adroit, guarded, exploratory, cutting, her hands held the secrets of every ambition and passion in the hearts and minds of men. Bl's abdomen covered yet bore through the drapes of the garments. The shoulder blades angled down like the wings of God's most precious angels, softly sleeping, giving way, fading, becoming, reincarnate, birthed in the outward curves of her lower back, complete in every way. Her upper chest fell, continual sweeping in slow motion to the outward, downward rounds of her upper breast. Back again, like the long slow shore, the breast reunited with her erect, elegant torso. They did not see, but the garment did, the rippling, taunt, ultimate core slightly pulsing to accept them.

Her back was unmentionable; to describe it is to sin. Though we are capable to try, some of God's creations deserve nor require acknowledgement from man to other men or to God himself.

"God is great, God is good, God is great, God is good, God is great, God is good..."

They were not aware, but still their minds and consciousness babbled at the upper skin of her back shone bare and the outline convergence of hips, buttocks and small of Bl's back in the soft beams of light.

The garment swayed against her slightly indented belly button, faintly showing the traces of the wide edges that disappeared as the edges slopped away from the garment and inward, foggily at first showing the limits of the indention and then finishing in a deep dark center; the loneliest place in existence.

"How long can you be truly alone? In the dark, devoid of senses, unable to see, hear or touch to the point where you even welcome danger just to have contact?"

Her lower abdomen, a compact picturesque navel full of slow roving waters and covered slops of earth, fallen bark, branches, twigs and leaves of every hue.

Bl knew, but they did not, how they craved. Her torso would be nothing but a priceless painting, fading outward along Bl's hips, round and spiraling like a misty dream to her inner thighs, slightly impressing upon her the faces of her private folds and down and around still to the backs of her knees.

The Garments hung to not reveal, but to give all of Bl's impressions of shape, form and expression. As much as they clung and flung and revealed, every impression of her flesh, every hint of its complete shape, texture, velocity, firmness, or softness, they and she became more and more singular and, as a composition, mysterious. Slight reveals as the garments swayed from her shoulders, about her torso and in her legs, gave familiar reminiscences with so many of them. They dialed back in their minds and forward in fantasy to something familiar or almost familiar like Bl.

Bl continued toward them to form the embrace. Bl's upper and lower legs, whose complete shapes were hardly discernible with no signs of effort, pushed and pulled the garment with the unity of our solemn promises to ourselves.

How do you describe legs, especially legs like these? Her calves showed their outer and upper curves against the garment's veil; the long flats of her thighs with many varying flats lit, shades and shadows, flowed down and pushed against the veil. Bl's slightly larger than the typical knees, were just as inspiring in mechanical function like her ankles, dutiful and efficient like a master chef in an active ornate kitchen preparing colorful delicacies. The garment's lower edges did not cover her lower leg. The skin reappeared after being covered from the neck, bosom and on down; this portion did not disappoint her other features, cylindrical, pyramidal similar to her torso, shafts giving height to Bl's eyes, leverage to the calves, thighs and feet. The wholesome utility daunting in purpose as necessary as a birth. The lower parts of her legs, if casted and bronzed, would be called Bl's.

Partially covering her feet, the chosen shoe added to her elegance, presence, purpose and power. The heel raised her just enough to display an elevated being, the coverings complimented the garment and accentuated the foot's skin, shape and purpose for the activity to be undertaken by Bl.

She would not have been there if she were not qualified. She earned the opportunity, the chance to perform.

"You are with me now," she said with her eyes as did they.

"You are with me now," together they said louder without words, but with every movement, gesture and expression swelled back to Bl. Bl would not peel off her clothes or grope herself, she would not frown, smile or raise her shoulders more than appropriate, but she did respond.

"You are with me now," almost questioning now with her mouth about to part and eyes pleading.

Bl turned unexpectedly, twirling so slightly and gracefully and again facing…slowly raising her left arm and hand soon followed with force, her right igniting herself. Bl's hands extended as far as she could reach, fingers tight, further to ignite, then she spread her fingers, backlit and bright rays streamed across the breadth of the space.

They could not and would not contain themselves any longer; they roared out with the energy of their commitments, their anxieties, their fears, their fantasies and their anticipations. Bl met the roars and trembles with the beginning.

∽

To get to this point required Bl's immense preparation. She had trained for years from childhood through adolescence. After reaching maturity, she relentlessly studied the past events like hers. Bl developed the ability to fast, her body, finding that balance needed to perform the event without the interference of bodily physical needs, wants and desires. She was ready.

Bl gave visual clue by beginning while lowering her arms slowly, aligning her hands with her shoulders. They responded slowly, retracting the roar and replacing it with attentiveness. She sang with the rhythm of the worlds. Every creature within her vocal grasp found relevance in her notes. An even captivating voice travelled to and through them, touching and patting on its way, calming them, offering to them and challenging them. "Solace," their insides yelled in response. Bl knew that this would be the favorite part.

Bl's maintained her outward gaze and began to pull the crowd's warm, moist air. First, over her nostrils the tingling follicles further spark her excitement, then she breaks the bond of her lips pulling larger amounts of air power deep into her lungs. The air compresses more and more, creating additional space for the inflow, air pushing into the lung walls saturating her capillaries with oxygen and moisture. Bl's upper body swells to contain the air.

"I have never pulled that much in before," Bl calibrated quickly, knowing that this made her more ready for the event.

There was no silence; the anticipation of the slow voluminous pull amplified them even more as it started to occur. Before Bl completed her initial pull, some of them having expended so much energy and effort to respond waned away, exhausted and drunk with exuberance, fainted, but forced themselves to keep their eyes open in an attempt to see her.

It was the middle of the day in Pri's land. She and her family had spent the last few days preparing to participate in Bl's event. "Pri, are you up, honey?" Pri's mother said as she opened the entrance to her resting area.

"Just like so many days, but earlier in the morning," Pri's mother reflected with quick anticipation of entering Pri's room to either find her still asleep with the alarm sounding or Pri having scampered to eat leaving the bed undone, the lights on and toiletries left open where they were last used and, of course, with the alarm still sounding.

Though they had prepared for Bl's event with required fasting, over resting, the special exercises and meditation, she still expected Pri to still be asleep. She wasn't, the bed was immaculately made for the first time in months; Pri's entire area was spotless. The mother, after being pleased with the sight, moved into the middle of the space and slowly twirled around on both heels proud of Pri's effort and looked approvingly, slightly raising her chin, the short downward curve of her cheekbone profile in Pri's recently cleaned mirror.

"She must be eating," her mother thought.

The mother moved to get her, but when she found Pri, Pri was not eating. Pri was making the final preparations for the entire family to participate in Bl's event. The mother was very satisfied with Pri in that she, much earlier than what would have been expected, was responding to the event in this way. She turned her attention to the other family members entering the space to participate in Bl's event. They all came in and took up places to watch the projections and recreations of the event. They, like the many others that could not be at the arena, would participate alone or in small groups or inside large arenas. Millions upon millions participated much the way high demand sports were once viewed, but with improved interactivity and realism.

"Pri," the mother called, slightly commanding.

"There is no need to thank me, Mum," Pri responded without really acknowledging her mother's presence.

The mother said to herself, "She calls me Mommie."

Bl began to let go. Without pushing, relieving or modulating the pressure of holding the air allowed Bl to siphon and bend the air up through her lungs, pulling moisture and air from her flesh and organs, throat, mouth and lips at her command to produce wide ranges of sounds and sound effects with sometimes very distinct and sometimes very subtle differences. The initial sounds she made shattered into their understanding. Bl eased them away from being totally aware of their screams with low constant and visceral sounds, rolled in from deep within her.

Bl glided across the performance area where the song could be experienced. The slight hints and accents confronted viewers asking them to judge.

"Am I enlightening, set-apart, special, yet pleasing, new and refreshing?"

"Yes! Yes! Yes...," they responded by the millions and millions; the sounds echoing from the many arenas, homes, individual receptors, offices and so on gave notice to anyone that was not participating. The next event would have a broader impact, and the world will be changed manyfold over.

"Seeeee..."

It came across like the most beautiful word ever sung, rising and falling, telling a story along the way, being consumed, individually interpreted for relevance and meaning. The initial word pierced and then rolled out, cutting space, time and bending understanding, home to its meaning. Bl caressed them, even like a constant hum with the first word; rolling out for the initial three minutes.

The hum held and held the listeners. Some listened intently without the slightest distraction; focused, yet without patience but a checked exuberance.

Bl continued, slowly compressing her body in a way to conserve the power to project, yet balanced with enough force to maintain the effect.

Into the first hour, Bl held note and force, "eeee...."

With ever so tiny inflection, speed and tone, Bl altered the constant hum with each change resonating so deeply in individual ways into the unique hearts of man, woman and child.

The word challenged some into drunken meditation and got them to the bottom of every question. Where an avoidance was built on fear, it was met with mental resolution that existence is undefined and therefore there was no reason to fear. It got them to the bottom of every anxious hope where there was only faith and not knowing. Bl demonstrated practiced truth to cure them. They were moved to the point of seeing what they had been trying not to see, and it coaxed them into confronting the formerly unseen hindrances in their lives.

Others embraced the word where it served as reaffirmation and assurance that what they saw and heard was good, nourishing, and dependable; cascading and crashing in teary faces of the many participants.

"It does not see..."

'It and see' held with similar inflection and brilliancy into the rich abyss of the event.

Bl moved with no track of time like her deepest emotions, know no time, like a purification. The rhythm outlasted any bad motivations, held over indulgence and temptations, the millions felt refreshed and surrendered.

Bl found her pace. They knew the meaning of her words that they had anticipated for so long now; hearing them brought believers and non-believers alike down. Having lost the control of their legs, they harmlessly fell about each other, languishing in the innocent, abundant physical contact.

"It does not need..."

"It" held and held and held. It seemed like a full night's swaying-so-lovely dance and 'need' again pierced and echoed for hour after hour after hour. Bl's face coming together as she paused all unnecessary bodily movement; it morphed in constant beauty, the eyes, the skin, the bones' movements, teeth and mouth composed a variety of emotions and meanings; with the last bit of emphasis on the end of the word 'need' added effect and explanation. The calm focused look of imperial place, arrival and motherly responsibility.

"It does not breathe…"

Bl mastered the ceremony technology that assisted her. The breathing techniques that she had practiced, learned, mastered and remastered using her lungs in an un-syncopated inhale-exhale partnership where one lung inhaled while the other exhaled and then the lungs would switch roles giving Bl and the other performers a constant flow of air to be used to annunciate their sounds and words.

The performers used the WOG device to assist them. Through the use of the WOG device and the mastery of the breathing techniques of song, the performers were able to accomplish astonishing feats of performance. The breathing allowed the performers to use very little amounts of air at a time since the body was constantly refreshed by the inhaling lung. The slow breathing allowed them to hold notes and gave them much more range of manipulation in the most subtle parts of any enunciation. The WOG device was a lightweight, hands-free attachment that gave super amplification to the performers' notes. Without the WOG, Bl's sounds would have been totally undetectable to those of hearing abilities, but with the WOG and the supporting transmitting and broadcasting systems, the performances were only limited by the amount of training and commitment of the performers.

"It does not bleed…"

The many notes, Bl joined them and took control; she overwhelmed them with her beauty, her presence, her talent and her performance.

—Precipice—

Forest, Part III

Moments calm, stolen away, mates, constant hum, necessitates, the trees, beasts, sects, and the tiniest all yell, ecstasy, rebel, the shadow, wind, rain, pain, birth sex again, again, again.

Clear, just dry, still gentle breeze, clearing, pruned, opened and free, branch, needle, fiddles, gorging swaying unison dance in the spree.

Forever stands, bending, quake, wind blast, light, present and hell the commands, the shape, shadows glides, crypts, nooks, nests, scurrying escapes, canopy fan blades.

Beam rivals, light, brilliant streaks, colored eyes, rushes down, filter forest dye, they fry, faint panting, fire consumed and die.

—The Game—

The low hum of the arena ignited into a sudden roar. The roar shook everything within considerable distance from the game. Lii reached a little startled for her father's hand as they got a little closer to the outside of the immense and, what was to her, a fantastic building.

The stadium was not new, but the structure's general aesthetic features found new life in their time. Its materials were the most durable and efficient to use for structure and the building's skin, which added a monochromatic impact to the foundation to the various decks and flying walls as well as the major supports. In the city, it held comfortably like a timeless precious jewel. Its flickering lights and sweeping planes were almost natural like that of shrimp shells or the fans of lobster tails with overlapping functional spaces that were all held tightly together by the overall composition that was meant to entice, process, embrace and release.

Lii walked with a little less speed as the roar came again seemingly at the very moment the light popped from the structures cuts and folds. Her father matched her pace.

Every roar came in almost perfect unison and died down with an even calming and lowering of energy. Lii and her father continued their approach. Her father wanted Lii to arrive at the game at this time.

Lii started to wonder as they continued toward the arena. She held her father's hand, wondered more and she moved without thinking about it, just kind of gliding along. This was her first time to the arena and the game and even though she had heard lots about it, she was still very excited and anxious about the experience of the game.

The game's participants took sides and competed against each other. The individual players were highly skilled in some cases and in some cases, were volunteers that committed themselves to playing.

A sensation, a new sensation, a new sensation immediately overcame Lii. She couldn't stop it, even if she could shut down all of her senses at once. The sensation entered her through every medium. The vibration of the roar passed through the ground, underneath and into her feet and up through her lower body. The sound with the same speed and magnitude hit like a gust, and then the energy of the people rushed over her, blowing out her clothes, permeating her skin, soaking into her muscles and bones. She was not the same.

In response to the sudden rush, Lii, not wanting to break their approach, held her pace well, but let out a little cough in reaction. Her father took slight notice, reflecting on her recent episode with a little illness, and assured himself that she was alright and continued their way.

As she glided along, Lii thought, "They all were sparked into cheer. There must be thousands and thousands of people in there."

Lii turned her head up and toward her father. He was focused on getting them there. She looked back between them and got the best angle that she could find to get the most distant field of view out to the city.

"…and thousands and thousands more," her thought continued. "How can a single act be so powerful? They cheer, they care."

Lii erupted into peak expression. She could hardly wait to experience the game for the first time. She had many questions at this time, but decided to wait and to not ask her father, but to let the experience unfold so that she would possibly be pleasantly surprised through the evening.

They entered the arena at the very top echelons of the structure whereby they could clearly see the full breadth of the mass of spectators and the participants. The game was fast. The fast-moving participants, full of color and energy, traversed back and forth, jockeying for position and advantage. Every break of the game was met with roaring reaction from the members of the crowds. The crowd did not wear colors to support either team and did not seem to specifically cheer for one team more than the other. The crowd cheered more in response to fantastic acts or feats accomplished by individuals or groups of individuals. The sound and physical contact of the game was highly noticeable to the spectators, and Lii was no exception. She absorbed the sights and sounds of the arena and the game.

The game carried through where play was not paused for mistakes or penalties, but points were awarded to the other teams or players were just removed from play or substituted. The players would play sometimes for days and days, especially when they were on a roll or if they were having a string of successes in the game. Long ago, even before Lii's father's childhood years, the game was commenced as a constant endeavor as constant as time itself. The teams would rotate in coaches or players as the rules permitted, but kept a competing team on the field. At such a time when a change of venue was desired and needed, new sets of staff, coaches and teams would be on stand-by and ready to begin play just as play would stop in another location.

The games were hosted in many places and in almost every country of the world. Locations began to take on game themes, and the games began to take on certain characteristics of play depending on the country or the location of the game. Even when through, the game was constant and endeavored to be a never-ending contest; the cities and event planners would from time to time perform routine or ritualistic preliminary events as precursors to certain game anniversaries in recognition of special events or accomplishments that were made in the preceding era or during more recent times in the games.

The players were managed with the most restorative processes to enable them to compete at the highest levels for extended periods. The biological advancements coupled with the advancements in bio-chemistry and synthetic dietary supplements created enormous players. As players rotated out of play, they underwent the usual restorative scans and run-ups, completed the necessary rest and leisure activity cycles until their next time in.

The records were staggering. One player held the record for most consecutive productive days. This award went to the player who obviously played for days and days and also made significant contributions to the outcome of the standing score or the score for a certain time period. The player played for a month. The team designations never changed. It was one side against the other, and both teams stood for wholesomeness, good and competitive exhibition. During one stretch, the gold team held a huge point spread advantage for at least five years. The blue team was never going to be able to come back if it were not for a couple of notable adds to the Blue Team's roster.

The Blue Team gained Ni. Ni experienced the game for the first time much like Lii experienced it. Ni was a spectator that had accompanied her father to the game. Ni was overtaken by the experience, excitement and widespread participation. The game was played in the arena, but spectators enjoyed the game by the millions from all over. Since the game was always on, anyone at any time could watch or go to the arena to catch it live. Ni immediately knew that she wanted to be a participant. After she and her father spent a considerable amount of time, they left totally exhausted from the excitement, the cheering and the energy of the game. Ni told her father on the way home that she wanted to be a competitor in the game.

Ni immediately was put into the training program to prepare the game's participants to play. She, of course, was a natural. Her natural abilities were matched with the finest developmental techniques of the times as she matured, playing in the training games. For reasons that no one could really identify and that she never disclosed, Ni chose to play for the Blue team, often caricatured in the team mascot. Her debut in the real game served to announce the coming trend of things to come with her truly exceptional career of accomplishments and records.

Ni, while on rest and leisure time, was able to travel. She decided after so much competition and being on display that she should just strike-out and just give in to whatever she felt like doing. After all, she was a very accomplished and well paid player who at a relatively early part of her career, had accomplished many records in the arena.

"I haven't been to Turkey," Ni concluded as she cycled through the many places that she had been.

The places that she had not been to by far outnumbered the places that she had been to, but something intuitive or innate led her there. Since her last play was in a major city, she quickly decided to not spend her leisure time in a major city. At this point, she decided that a little research could come in handy.

"I am not totally a free-spirit," she added to her growing excitement, anticipating the residing of the feelings of post-muscular exertion and being away from her routine of prep and play.

＊

Ni pulled up the geography and facts; the geographical real time and historical information was more fun she decided as she laid back and let the information cascade past her. Being an athlete, her conscious-ness gravitated to the mountainous and challenging terrain. Her body reflected on what it would be like to train in some of the more remote cliffy areas. She zoomed in and out, peeling through the green layers, getting close-ups of meandering mountain trails, roads disappearing and reappearing due to low use periods, rolling hills, cliffs, roving waters. Ni panned away from the built-up areas, to the towns, observing the people in their various activities, coming and going, farming, having recreation, crafts people practicing their skills, children interested in the livestock and more interested in the mud and so on.

The smile brimmed in her as the children raced along with the penned baby beasts, muddy and competing first to the pole, attempted trips, ground dips, the child shirt rips. Spins again, the child looks back ever so briefly, brightly into Ni's eyes, matching Ni's smile teeth for teeth widening across the sky and landscape and then back to the heat, beating boys, beasts and pen. Ni bubbled up to full laughter.

"I feel better about the future. These kids are going to carry the day later."

"It's something how one good laugh can make an entire vacation," as she panned past the village.

"My eye seems to like the trails. My mind likes the sense of move-ment, the recorded and maintained trodden form expressed over time. My sense of exercise, exertion, flow and encounter passing through or around the various gathering places of people or shading areas for an-imals or hunting departure points," Ni thought.

She knew that she was excluding the cities, the mountains, the cliffs, the towns, the markets of the past or the high tech dwellings and con-veyance apparatus of the present.

"Why do I like these things more than the others?"

She recognized that her decisions to travel and to find a destination would be different from others or from other athletes of the game.

"Others would be drawn to or interested in the villages or just the peaks or just a certain craft of the people."

⁂

Ni drifted in reminiscences to the other trails, tries and fails of the encounters of training and tries. Ni's face worn of water and want led through and to the legs said, "Is laughter a word?" The Keeper offered. Without saying it, but meaning it, the Keeper's action said, "Don't answer that," and then burst into, just below haunting, not quite hysterical laughter.

"Why do all the Keepers laugh so?" Ni thought and thought again.

"The Keepers must be the happiest people in the world because they are always laughing."

The laughter usually meant that you were either being stupid, or it was about to be proven how stupid you were by comparison."

Ni continued to think, beginning to understand like not before but in that moment, that instant of understanding when everything changes, once understood cannot be un-understood crept into Ni like a poison. Ni felt to spout out in tenacity, with the new understanding.

"The nuance of the laughter, sometimes it's ridicule, sometimes it's prelude," Ni concluded.

"This time it was definitely prelude."

The Keeper in traditional dress, like a contemporary western sub-Saharan African, minor ceremonial garb put Ni at ease with the end of the laughter and began to immediately get to the point of the training encounter.

"Of course, you know the Bible." Ni felt like the Keeper was look-ing for a response of validation, but at the same time not needing it and felt to suddenly spout-off a quote or interpretation to kind of agree with the Keeper.

Ni remembered the urgency of the need to get by this Keeper with-out having to go back or to start over at any point, and the Bible verses that may have been appropriate for the moment cycled-up into Ni's forethought, without being said, in attempt to provide a witty response. Ni, having learned that speaking out of turn usually does not lead to success, kept silent, but held thoughts ready like a bulwark against the advance of a surely overwhelming force.

"You are great Ni and if it wasn't for that dark skin, you would be as close to perfection as possible," the Keeper stated.

"Where does greatness come from and what does it matter? The body, we, must be pushed and pushed and developed and developed, why?"

Ni never heard the word 'why' delivered with so much force of meaning and in isolation. It was not like the wind and was not like a thunder clap, but more like the satisfying sound of confidence as it was a small display of the Keeper's voice control and power.

"Ni, remember, learn to control one thing, you can control many things, learn to have power with one thing, and you can have power with many things."

Ni knew not to answer. The Keeper continued, knowing that Ni would not speak.

"Is there one vessel? What is a vessel? Is the Bible a vessel?" the Keeper took a glance at Ni while questioning.

Ni, stationary, eyes locked, senses at a heightened state, almost in full receiver mode took account of the Keeper as well. They flashed over each other, head to toe, the miles, the wear, the adjustments, the commitment, the enduring, the years, the mistakes told the tales of their plights and fights. Impressed, the Keeper continued, realizing that Ni was ready.

Ni didn't utter some off irrelevant verse and did not re-question just to hide the unknowing. Ni held that kind of aura where submission was clear, but it came at a price.

The Keeper continued again, "The game is like a vessel where the body, our bodies, get better and better, faster, quicker, stronger, more resilient. A carrying vessel should and usually does have an origin and a destination.

The thought of destination caught Ni off guard. Ni did not speak, the slight shift in body position and redistribution of weight showed it all.

"Your greatness is not in vain Ni, do not worry," the Keeper started to put Ni at ease.

"Like millions before you, you have cancer and the cancer will end your career and end your life here."

Ni, having adjusted not so long ago, did not adjust again, at least, on the outside. Being told that with certainty, that you are going to die, is a different place, a precipice.

"If I am lucky, I have it too," the Keeper confessed while letting Ni know that the journey was not to be made alone.

"All of them, Ni," the Keeper, not yelling, but with emphasis told Ni.

All of them, the most deadly to the apparently curable, run-of-the mill sickness elevating the voice to offer that the word sickness was meant with sarcasm.

"Remember the sphere, Ni, remember the possibilities, remember the keys and remember where the truth, the truth does not rest but hums, pulsating the one and only flow of fulfillment, an endless destiny. When was the first cancer, quote unquote, discovered? When Ni?" the

Keeper now firmly challenging Ni and cementing the status of the Keeper over the unproven.

"Where? Why? How?"

Ni retraced all that could be traced through all of the training, all of the experiences and all of the travels and Keepers up until now and quickly concluded that the answers were not there.

"The evolution of our species has been...," the Keeper trailed off, fading and pausing and then continued. "...misunderstood. The planetary system that we have held, studied, loved and sustained ourselves will be gone."

"You know your Bible," the Keeper affirmed to both of them.

"It's gone. Now what?"

Ni knew the spiritual and felt that that was enough.

"In the face of extremely virulent bacteria and small creatures capable of living for years without any external nourishment and under extreme conditions, we regard these largely as our enemy."

Ni was getting it now. The Keeper motioned with a glance to Ni to not get too comfortable and continued to talk.

"The bacteria, the small creatures, the cancer cells, stronger than any one of us...," the Keeper did not have to finish the thought.

"My God," Ni's face said it all.

Ni was changed again forever. The Keeper paused and lowered the demeanor and rested, purposefully lowering the eye level below Ni's. Ni did not have to realize the cue to speak and did.

"Cancer is the...our next phase of evolution. Is it not stronger, is it not made of our essence, is it not purposeful? At this point, getting to the next inhabitable planet is outside of our survivability. We keep thinking to put our own kind on other planets, but we should be thinking to put our evolved essence on other planets. There are all kinds of cancers and extreme bacteria and small creatures."

Ni put the pieces together like a confident child with an oversized puzzle. The Keeper kept pace with Ni's thought, logic and words and did not interject, but joined Ni.

"The evolutionist," the Keeper snarled with the distaste of a measly meal that was the only one available.

"The Harvards, Oxfords and the rest of them. Yes, we need them and yes, they are important, but let's just take evolution for example. Harvard was meant to be Harvard and the like was meant to be the like. Harvard or the like could have easily been your destination Ni," the Keeper said to keep the discussion personal.

"Don't feel so bad about it, Ni. If you dream well here, you will dream well after."

The Keeper went back to the subject. "Why would evolution be confined to one time? Forget the tolerance of the nearest inhabitable planets. If we evolved once, we can evolve again. But this time, maybe with being more informed, armed, equipped etc. with all of the best that we have to offer in terms of philosophy, science, technology; we can supply the next worlds with the survivable evolutionary primordial microbes to save our race. Forget finding the perfect planet. Embrace the cancers, do the subcellular engineering, build the microbes and take some damn chances."

The Keeper was getting out of character with spikes of emotion, revealing caring, but with caring comes a little uncertainty, Ni observed.

"These same Harvards, Yales, and MITs just like the INs, calculate the crap out of ancient problems, but go home and play poker, taking chances with the stakes where the stakes are lots less. We have the real stakes and the Order does not forget this. We know about certainty, but do not practice the principles of certainty in dealing with the most important initiative in the history of the race, extinction. Extinction of the good, the vessel, the temples of truth and righteousness' victory over evil, you see?" the Keeper asked with affirmation.

"What about the targets in space?" asked Ni.

"What about them?"

"What are the probabilities that some so-called advanced civilization would not be able to detect, track and retrieve our launches? You could do a lot worse with a billion dollars."

Ni wanted the pieces to lock into place. "Where is this happening?" Ni asked, leaping to the conclusion of the experimentation and performing of what the Keeper described.

"Think about the Amazon, the aboriginal lands, the American Indian burial grounds and other forbidden locations, buildings, and then think again."

The Keeper realizing the finality of the thought saw it in every stretch of skin on Ni. Ni, did not slump, did not sadden and was not joyed. The Keeper added, "There are seldom happy truths, Ni."

⁂

Ni panned back to real time and as a feeling that was akin to a mix of boredom, exhaustion and that feeling that you get when faced with so many choices where one choice is not obviously better, and a speck of clarity pops into your mind and the room. The speck seemed to quiet the surroundings around her even more into a deeper mental solace of satisfaction.

"I will go to that nearby city at the base of the hills of the mountains, travel out to these systems of trails and take off for my vacation out off the trails and away from the game."

⁂

Lii was thrilled and thrilled again by the remarkable circus-like abilities of the game's participants. They were obviously skilled differently and had different abilities, but their skills and psychical characteristics complemented each other to form cohesive comprehensively effective teams. Lii, even at her young age, noticed how the different players' abilities served the overall combined activity of the team much like other early sports, but in a highly-refined way for the highly refined participants.

They had prepared to attend the game in person, and Lii's father wanted Lii as well as himself to be part of the experience of longevity of the game; after all, this was the core principle of the game. It's constant, it's competitive, everywhere it effects everyone and everything and yet, there is a winning team; ahead at the time, but unknown if there will be an outright winner one day.

Now not a maiden, but a maiden's age, Lii sought to continue, plan and develop as a growing young woman should. The mother did not push back against her connection with her father. As a young girl, Lii spent more time in the garage than she did in the kitchen. She was still very much feminine but had picked up her father's gestures and expressions and a few curse phrases. All the physical activities resulted in Lii being a very well developed, muscular, young princess, yet with short finger nails and hands with a few nicks.

Lii and her companion obliged to be alone, companion first, "slow down, no need to rush, she knows why we are here."

Lii, never late, arrives, everything set, hammer, pliers, screwdriver, apron and box, dropped, oily, but clean, clanked, chinked and hammer thud on the wood and carpet floor.

"Lii, honey, why did you bring all of your stuff in the bedroom?"

"My father said don't go anywhere without your tools."

—Haven—

"Isn't life good?" Gni said as if to keep talking. To Smpi the question was new, but the meaning was escapingly familiar. Smpi let the basic question roll around inside her head like a marble on packed sand.

"So basic," she thought.

Gni was inviting her, "But to what?"

Smpi responded to offer an invite of her own, "not always" intentionally avoiding the basic premise of what is to come.

"Well," Gni, almost commanding, now offering a little intensity with her eye-contact toward Smpi. "Are you going to answer what I said?" Smpi offered back with more avoidance.

"No," said Gni. "Isn't it good?" Gni continued. "We are so able. When healthy and of good spirit we can do worldly and unworldly things. As we review the history of time, we have become a better and better people despite the seemingly unconquerable challenges that have risked our development, future and existence."

Smpi was proud that she had gotten Gni to go further.

"As best we can tell, most of the things that hinder our good health and spirit are products of our own making," Gni explained further. "So, isn't life good?

"Are all the times when it's not good our fault?" Smpi debated back, building her case to refute the premise.

"But tell me, Smpi, is it good, at least in general terms?" Our bodies are miracles in resilience, endurance, aesthetics and utility. And our minds? Good heavens. Now we know that we cannot began to imagine the advancements and the accomplishments of our prodigy. We have come so far and have so far to go.

"Can't we go backwards?" Smpi asked. Not liking that she had to inject that thought.

"Of course, we do it all of the time. We go back and have to learn the lessons of the past. In a way, this is progress in that it reaffirms the very progress that has been forgotten or ignored. I am sure you understand that," Gni paused, but did not observe for reaction reaffirming that she had brought her point home.

"Would you like to sing about the cancers?"

There was no answer. The moment seduced both to naked adornment of place and grace. "Chasity, Forest, Precipice, For Us...need I go on? I will anyway...The Game, Passion, Core. Undeniable," Gni purposefully finished with Undeniable asking and again, ascertaining, at the same time, true to Keeper form.

"So much is said in silence and stillness."

"What does the still silent stone face of the mountain or the forest void of humankind say?"

"So, you are saying that even when we are at our worst, it's ultimately good for civilization?" Smpi concluded.

"I didn't say civilization, but since you mentioned it, I would say that I have to agree. You're a bright chimp, Smpi. Now stop being coy and answer. No, never mind, let's move on. Why is life good?"

Now Smpi, after laughing a little, said, "Wait."

"No, let's not wait," Gni pushed. "That's part of going back, isn't it?"

Smpi did not feel so smart. She felt embarrassed in that she appeared to have figured it out, but did not communicate the answer in a manner that said that she had known the information for a long time and that she was very familiar with it. Instead she sounded like the wanton upstart that she was.

"Gni is so smart," she affirmed.

"If I am so smart, why are you lecturing to me?" A little of the embarrassment began to harden into shame.

"Let's stick to the subject. Besides, you can only handle one of these at a time," Gni said back.

Smpi quickly pondered, "I can protest that slight insult, or I can let her go and see what she has to offer."

Smpi let Gni go on. Smpi adjusted her posture on the sofa, involuntarily showing Gni the front of her body. Smpi sensed that Gni was going to end her questioning and move to informing her, teaching her, exposing her. Smpi felt defenseless.

"Why 'one of these?' What did she mean, or did she let that slip?" Smpi's curiosity did not push her to interject much more.

She knew that whatever it was that Gni meant for her to get, that she was going to get it, square in the face. She was defenseless.

Gni's voice dropped down to an even cadence, almost monotone, with slight inflictions that coupled with the strengths on her face as she spoke on certain things. It was almost procedural like she was talking from memory with a little paraphrasing salted in.

"The Pyramids are not some folly story of the most educated people in the world of that time and competitive by today's standards, building skyscrapers to appease themselves and their Kings, Queens or Pharaohs. And they are certainly not some insertion from beings from another World. Oooh, Aliens, advanced space creatures, Pniteos? And they're going to come back one day and get us! Oooh!" Gni joked, and she played the part of a scared little girl looking out the window afraid and up at the mid-day sky and then back to Smpi. But Smpi was scared.

"Gni's animations? The timing? How did she know?" Smpi asked herself, her face giving hints of her thoughts.

"Gni," Smpi called out slightly, raising out of the cushions; she wanted her to stop.

Gni kept talking, raising her open hand toward Smpi to stop her interruption. It worked. Smpi first relaxed her shoulders, let her hands spread back over the suede surface, lowering her body back down, keeping her eyes on Gni. Smpi knew that she was losing control.

Rhetorically, Gni continued, "The Adviis used to ask why did these ancient intelligent people, in all of their brilliance, invest the enormous resource for the sake of, even the most special, tomb? It doesn't add up, not even close, and it doesn't make sense," Gni began to answer her own Adviis question.

Smpi thought with slight disengagement, "That was a leap."

Smpi had followed Gni, but now, she wasn't so sure. A leap that Smpi would soon learn about.

"The realization of lack of knowledge and understanding."

"How could I have been so...," she didn't have the courage to complete the sentence.

Smpi's mind, instead of accelerating with curiosity, began to resign and to allow Gni to see her void.

"No, not for tomb!" Gni sounded off with a little practiced, well-timed frustration. "Not solely a tomb. But the tomb serves two purposes. First, the idea of having the grandest of tombs supported the mass belief in the hierarchical social system where the Royal Families were held in collective high esteem and were worshipped as descendants of Deities. The masses believed that they, themselves, the masses, were blessed to have been given 'Deities' to watch over them. They felt safe. Having a grand tomb was… ," Gni paused. "A natural progression, not to mention the construction being great for the economy—the people bought in," Gni concluded.

"They resigned themselves," Gni made a quick check over Smpi. "To the power of Kings, Queens and Pharaohs."

They resigned? Did she know? How could she have known, but she did know. Smpi let her face drift away from Gni, but her facial tension and wide eyes showed that she was still fully engaged with Gni.

Gni completed her check as Smpi's resignation darkened into hopelessness.

Gni continued, "Secondly, remember that this was the most advanced people, after recording their history where future kingdoms with greater achievements, were considered inevitable. The wise taught, and the Royals listened. Their mortality was evident. The Royals joined in."

Smpi listened to the point where Gni's voice blanketed her from all outside stimuli. Every statement of understanding filled her, but it came with more and more regret. Smpi's mind retracted further into reverse-synopsizing a mental fasting state.

"Yes, they resigned," Smpi agreed in her mental shadows, her body, already weak, panted toward malfunction.

"One last gift to the people that I love and that my ancestors have loved as parents love their children. This was so obvious," Gni dictated, still in verse with her recital.

"They could have easily sent their royals off with great fiery ceremonies or used lesser structural means. But no, the pyramids were intentional, everything from the application of the most advanced math, science and technologies to the sleek marble like coating of the glistening sides of the perfect forms; they represented a balanced civilization where accomplishments were tempered with morals and purpose and societal buy-in. The pyramids epitomized the existence of the moral and physical ideas of their race, entombed the Deities for safe keeping and passage into the future. Of course, the passage was not meant to be physical, like you hear so many clowns, so called academics, espouse about. The passage was representational and instructional and it worked!"

Smpi felt Gni's amplified voice close around her.

Gni continued, "Why did ancient civilization combine so much of their resource, history and their most precious beings into a message for the future? Were they allowing future generations of civilizations to look upon their works, investigate their culture and practices and to decide if they wanted to adopt their ways?"

Smpi stirred a little upon hearing this as if to concur with what appeared to be another one of Gni's stated facts. Gni's face fixed from routine and infrequent tenseness to a purposeful flat seriousness.

"No, Smpi, they did not," Gni added with more audibility.

"It seemed like a natural progression," Smpi thought.

"No, Smpi," Gni belted out again. "The Egyptians did not offer a choice; they knew that if given a choice, so many of us would choose wrong. They left the world with nowhere to go but in one direction. They dictated to the future! They dictated to the world of then and dictated to the civilizations to come that, you will know us. You will know our accomplishments, you will know our values and by knowing these things, you will tend to perpetuate the good that they represent in this world. The pyramids are beyond ignorable and undeniable messages to the future. Of course, the messages are not crammed down our throats nor were the ideas to undertake the projects crammed down the throats of the citizens. The messages were created and allowed to spread and flourish through direct impact, but more so through indirect means where second, third, fourth and fifth…tenth and so on effects would have exponentially expanding impact. Science begat better science, better science leads to lateral improvements, infinite other fields. For those that say that science, for example, can easily be turned to do harm, I say an oak tree does not grow from date tree seeds."

"The composition was excellent," Smpi knew it.

"All of my training, all of my independent pursuits where I have excelled or not excelled, all of my desires and lack of desire, all of my accomplishments have taken me so far from the truth."

Smpi's reflected on perhaps a chance to hold on, after all, now she knew the truth as told by Gni. Her future would be painted forever with shame and the sloth of her getting to the point in her life where she did not know what she should have known.

"I have missed so much," Smpi reflected back. "The truth, as monumental and momentous of thousands of years and as large and weighty as an example, needs to be looked back at by people and time like a moon in the sky."

Smpi forgot about holding on. When she let go, her inner glands released again, streaming their secretions into her brain. The brain self-fasted at a quicker and quicker pace.

"Gni," Smpi whimpered.

Gni, pacing the room, taking loose inventory of the room's possessions, again and again, strutted all around Smpi and continued her recital and did not nor want to hear her.

"Gni," a slight stronger whimper this time was met with equal ignorance. "Gni," Smpi said mournful, yet without the tears.

She turned her fading vision upwards somewhere beyond her pausing just long enough to catch a verse from Gni's incessant rolling and forced it closed, and the secretions permeated her nervous system. Her muscles and skin rolled with slow fading contractions, twitching around her eyes and cheeks. The roll subsided down to barely detectable pulses until she was almost gone.

"I'm sorry," came out like a slow long song of meditation, crescendoing and bottoming several times along the way with every letter, a new meaning, a new tear, a new grief, a new beginning, a new sound.

Gni's primary job was done, but not her recital. She had counted Smpi out sometime ago, when Smpi was a maggot, as she recounted in exacting detail the history of the Ancient World in that part of the country. She named the Kings, Queens and Pharaohs in succession, calling out their stand-out relatives, their lineages, their accomplishments, the highlights of their lives and their deaths. Gni, just like she was taught to do, painstakingly reviewed the conception, initiation, progress and completion of the major buildings, citing the architects, the engineers and the buildings' benefactors and their final mummified inhabitants, detailing the funerary process for each by highlighting only the differences in how the post-death procession ceremonies were conducted and concluded.

Gni continued to say what had to be said.

"Basically, as a measure, the goodness in life would have no value if it weren't for the existence of badness with, of course, the greatest badness being pure evil. The goodness of life is its own reminder that evil exists and that it has the capacity to engage us in struggle. And once we acknowledge the existence of the struggle, the meaning of the good life becomes clear. You see, we often postulate that the struggle as told in a guiding book is spiritual, yet more of our world. No, again, I say no."

"Our God, who art in Heaven...my God, 'art in Heaven,' who are you kidding? I don't think so. Our God, yes, but our God has not vanquished evil; our books agree. Our God is and has been forever, it seems, in a pitched battle, a super-galactic war that has been occurring in every dimension: physical, spiritual, the thought dimension, the dimensional seams and voids between dimensions and so on. We use the word war, (She recalled, the teachings of the Adviis) because it is the most comparable activity to compare it to, but it is not really comparable to what is happening. The clashes at the super sub-atomic level number in the billions. Ten, twenty, a million times over, are syncopated with the collisions of galaxies, of beings physical and non-physical and individual spirits within themselves, the billions of wars waged in a thick, deep, endless whirling soup of conflict."

Gni, still in verse, self-admired her progress thus far and felt comfort in knowing that she would be flawless in her recital on to the end. A slight warm smile crossed her face in satisfaction that Smpi would not get the rest of the story, would not know the entire truth.

"God, in the midst of the conflict that laid waste to a dominant portion of existence…," Gni continued the recital, "delved into his mastery and command of the very existence that he fought and continues to fight for and created a haven. This haven on earth is the safe-keeping of the very basics of the force of good. The safe-keeping is like a time capsule, like a frozen gene-pair preserved for the future, an ark carrying the ways of good into the time when the struggle is complete and the evil is vanquished.

"Why can't we know the truth?" the Adviis would ask.

"We would not accept it. Much like the wise of the ancient times, the truth had to be presented in such a way to support its own survival, in a way that it is acceptable. God knew that only so many would believe the story of his Son and that mankind's beliefs would be fragmented and different; yet, there had to be binding, continual pressure to keep the nature of good sharp; these pressures come in the form of the tests that we endure and overcome with goodness and Godliness. Even when we embrace other belief systems, no one denies the nature of an erect masterpiece, the values, the motives, the absolutes that brought the masterpiece into being. The bindings of science, philosophy, mortality, love, procreation keep us like the spices, and bindings of the mummy keep the messengers. The stories and existence of Deities, and so on offers a no-lose situation for anyone to either decide against religion or for it, or embrace it. You acknowledge the existence of higher power, to refute it; you are pushed into the very bindings that the Lord has laid to preserve the good."

Gni turned to Smpi, both now in silence. After many hours and the passing of the light, darkness and all of the colors of the sky, Gni was totally exhausted. She felt a mixed sense of guilt, pity, accomplishment and extreme weariness. The Adviis called this unique feeling, that was only obtainable by completing the recital, the 'kee.' Gni surveyed the room once more and approached Smpi's limp and frozen gaze. The last ceremonial confirmation, a taste. Gni kneeled and moved to taste Smpi when she was totally shocked to hear a small stirring in the adjacent space.

Gni, shocked, quickly moved toward the sound and upon arrival met face to face with an innocent looking young male child, a child young enough to have strayed far enough away from his keepers in adventure, but old enough to know that what he may have witnessed was private and special. She closed the distance between them to look into his eyes. He was not afraid. She offered and then pushed her left index finger into his mouth, forcing him to taste Smpi. The boy never lost eye contact with Gni as his expression met hers in confirming that he had heard and understood the recital. She pulled out her finger. The boy turned his lips inward to finish every molecule of Smpi into his awareness.

Gni broke the silence, "I pledge and pray for God's eventual victory."

The boy responded, "It will surely come."

He walked past her on the way to examine Smpi.

"What is life?"

—Progenii—

Forest, Part IV

Eve, Edge of Eden, moments in the wake, reveals, real, which way or wanders, go, snow, flakes, drift, drift, drift stick, accumulate, shelters haze, fresh, countless graves She makes.

Piece by piece, tree withers regenerates, fate, souls of Man reincarnate, winter bitter freeze, shivers please, my children will not hear, pine, oak, apple, shrub, flower, grass and pear.

Again, a million cries, nature reigns, chains, cycle horrid chaos, pounds, slow hammer blows, once again muffles out the newborn sounds.

Walk back, eerie air, bare, comes the night, dusk, ash, the day, decay, the fight observed, felt, known the plight.

Child return, steps, specks, particles, pebbles, shift, found, fallen figments intermingle from the bushy, dense.

More than time, be mine, expands the breadth, distant boundaries, peaks, in glimpse, width and depth kept myth.

Cni busied himself with all of the prevailing problems. Smiling inside to the many that will fix themselves in due course and in due time.

"Don't worry too much along the way," Cni thought out to the others who did not know, did not know about Bl, Lii, VGR, or the campfire nights, the fights and precise.

"It is not for everyone, but it is for me," Cni thought about the eventuality of being a Keeper and the so many to come after.

Everything about Cni said, "complete." That feeling that, if you are lucky, you only get a few times in your life. No need to move left or move right knowing the outcome of the things that were previously a worry. The humor of the day, the security, relaxed body and mind.

"Right here," the sense of place took him back to the sphere, the maps, maggots, the proven, the unproven, the forest, the alive, the dead, the precipice. The immense satisfaction he knew the moment was bulging for. How many moments passed when it was not known to be now?

"…Hieroglyphics," The Giver threw it out there, neither a question and definitely not an answer. Not an answer that easy.

"The ass end of a hard lesson always tasted better anyway," thought Cni. Cni knew one was coming. Cni did not brace, but offered a little counterplay, like a reflex. Even to Cni's disbelief, he blurted the thought out and spoke it to the surrounding area, definitely not directly at the Giver, "You mean endgame." The Giver added and got back to it. "And the obelisks?"

Cni was used to the seeming jumps (Z) of topics that are not jumps, but are indeed connected. This was definitely not a trick question.

Cni cycled through the historicals, the countries of locations and as much as Cni could about the origins, symbology, orders of architecture, myths, and sculptures. Cni rattled off the few facts, countries, materials, heights of the shortest and tallest, their weights, orientations and colors.

The figures, animals, falcons, flowers, hawks, beetles, birds of prey, the astrology, the myths, cats, ants, antelope, beavers, tail, headdress.

The Giver observed and gleamed inside and demurred as well for knowing the hell that he'll...

"Nice try, but we'll get back to the history, meaning and impact of the headdress later," one of the Giver's favorite's topics.

"Sounds like a damn good move to me," Cni let the Giver know that it was not going to be all serious.

"Are there any hieroglyphics on the tallest or at the so-called great cathedrals for that matter?"

The Giver recited the mainstream and lesser known cathedrals, the names, the years of completion, the styles, the architects, the different characteristics and locations.

"Again, not a trick question?" Cni let the thought pass, transitioning to receiver mode.

"Eight Egyptian obelisks in Rome, other obelisks, Africa, Italy, France, Turkey, etc. Each with four sides and with varying amounts of hieroglyphic panels per side." The Giver stopped with a tone that did not ask, but wound out a response.

Cni resisted the resistance, like the "endgame" comment did not draw wrath, Cni's silence, nudged, askingly the Giver.

"What do they say? Are they symbols, stories, songs, prayers, or poems? Behind the question, knowing that Cni was done.

Cni was nearly perfect.

"... shots of unknown challenges, trials and viciously skilled enemies that would surely come and try the perfection," framed through the Giver's certainty of the future.

The Giver's mixed emotion, if you can call it that, began to seep out in the miniscule changes in demeanor; so far, the Giver knew that it was only detected by Cni in the subconscious, soon it will be clear. "Oh my dear Constantine."

To answer the question, Cni began to rattle off additional facts to provide introductory background to his answer.

"Cni was showing off," they both observed and agreed.

Cni spoke of the countries, the cities, the plazas, the piazzas and monuments, but then paused while coming to the understanding that the pattern being used was not going from East to West, North to South, paths of travel or any recognizable direction. Cni, of course, was exposed to enough of the symbology to assuage any further serious curiosity.

"The appeasing lie." Nothing more seductive than the truth.

The doubts of history spun and faded again; the training, pain, shame, gain, and the meanings remain.

Cni chuckled and shrugged in happy wonder about how it was, at this late time, that so much learning was still to be had.

Cni asked, "If am I going to leave here, as if on another "Proven" and rush to read the obelisks, in what order?"

-The Turkish Order-

P n i M K i Z y i C m i
R N i W b y n y L h a O
T i V g i F L G T L G V
G R F T L Y A Q i P l N
v B l P r i L i i N i G
n i S m p i C n i